# HOT AND COLD

# E. PRYBYLSKI

Scriptures taken from the Holy Bible, New International Version®, NIV®. Copyright © 1973, 1978, 1984, 2011 by Biblica, Inc.™ Used by permission of Zondervan. All rights reserved worldwide. www.zondervan.com The "NIV" and "New International Version" are trademarks registered in the United States Patent and Trademark Office by Biblica, Inc.™

Cover image designed by Angel Leya.
https://www.angeleya.com/

www.insomnia-publishing.com

ISBN: 9798987571910

*To Jason. My husband, my love, my partner in terrible puns.*

*To my sisters. You really are my fault.*

*To Chris and Jen. One of these days, I will get my revenge.*

If you enjoy this book, please leave a review wherever you purchased this book. Reviews help others find authors' books. It's more important than you know.

# CHAPTER 1

Winter in Boston is, at the best of times, unpleasant. If you have never been there in the cold months, the entire city becomes an icy traffic jam slashed by chill winds blowing in off the ocean. Living in the city during the cold months is miserable, but doing so while homeless is harder still. I don't recommend it.

I huddled deeper into the heavy jacket I wore as I left St. Mary's Church with Jim after helping him close up that night. At least it wasn't snowing or, worse, raining. Jim sighed, running his hand over his short hair in a gesture I'd picked up from him. I'd learned it meant he was frustrated or stressed about something. I used it in the same way.

"I'm sorry," he said for about the millionth time. "I wish I could let you stay on the couch, but Mrs. DeWit is—"

"Jim, it is all right." I squeezed his shoulder as we made our way across the parking lot to Jim's van. He opened the door and pulled out the wheelchair ramp, sliding it down to the pavement before he rolled himself up it and into the van proper.

A former Marine and the man in charge of organizing outreach at St. Mary's Church, Jim was my best friend. He was in his mid-thirties, human, and had light brown hair and brown eyes. Both legs below the knee had been amputated following some kind of explosion he'd been in during his military service overseas. Jim didn't talk about that, and I didn't ask. Social graces are not my strength and never have been, but even I knew when a subject was too painful. He had been my rock since the death of Father John the year before, and he, Dust, and Eirlas had stood with me against the demon responsible for Father John's murder.

Since being barred from staying at the shelter at St. Mary's the previous autumn, I had bounced around between a couple friends' homes. Father Demoyne, the current priest who had taken over for Father John, had decided I was unwelcome after I'd ended up a murder suspect. While I'd been cleared of that charge, he hadn't changed his mind. So I spent a night here or there on my friends' couches, but between nosy neighbors and the fact that Dust and Eirlas shared a one-bedroom apartment in a tightly monitored building, I could only stay so often or so long.

While there were plenty of other shelters, they weren't in parts of the city I frequented, which would have taken me far from any of the people I knew and the community I served. Beyond that, most of the ones nearest the church were for battered women, women with children, or people fighting with drug addiction. I was none of those things and refused to take resources from people who needed them more than I did. Being an angel, even a fallen one, I'm hardier than many of the various races on the planet and knew living rough wouldn't kill me. Even if I was cold, hungry, and miserable much of the time.

Instead, I had taken to staying with a group of homeless people camped beneath the Harvard Bridge. It was only a block or so from where Jim lived, and the bridge offered some measure of shelter from the weather. The proximity meant I could hitch rides to St. Mary's with Jim on the days he worked. And the days he didn't, he usually demanded I come by and at least use his shower and have a hot meal. In those ways, I was thoroughly blessed.

Jim grunted. "Least I can do is make sure you get something hot in your belly before you go. Come on." He transferred into his driver's seat and stowed his wheelchair before turning to face forward.

I rounded the van and climbed in, unzipping the heavy coat I'd taken from the donation bin. It didn't quite fit me across the chest, but it was one of the only jackets we'd received that had wing slits in the back, so if I needed to call my wings out, I could do it without risk of injuring myself or destroying my only winter coat. "I appreciate your help, Jim. But you do not need to worry about me so much."

"Don't."

I cocked my head.

"*Don't* need to worry so much. Remember your contractions."

Grunting, I shook my head. "You *don't* need to worry about me so much," I repeated. Even after almost two years on Earth, I struggled with the language at times. English is so much less formal than Enochian, and I still didn't have a particularly large vocabulary. Jim, Dust, and Eirlas had been working with me on it since they said the less strange I seemed, the more readily people would accept me. They were right, of course, but that didn't make it any less frustrating while I was learning.

Dust and Eirlas were also staff at St. Mary's. Dust ran the soup kitchen, and Eirlas managed the shelter proper. The two were the cutest orc-and-elf couple I'd ever seen. Well, to be fair, they were the only orc-and-elf couple I'd ever seen, but still. Either way, the two of them, along with Jim, comprised my very limited group of friends since my abrupt arrival in Boston. In fact, when I stopped to think about it, my fall had happened in March. With it now February, we were about a month away from that anniversary.

I glanced in Jim's direction. "My birthday is soon," I said, finding the word odd. As an angel, I hadn't really been birthed in the traditional sense, but it was as close as I'd ever come to finding the right word for it. Jim said it was customary to celebrate one's arrival in the world, and that was the word they used for it.

"Oh yeah. End of March, isn't it?" Jim smiled at me as he put the van in gear and drove toward his apartment. While we often took the T—the Boston Rail Transit System—to the church, when he ran his groups, he typically drove. He found it easier to bring all the things he took with him in his van than trying to juggle it in his lap on the subway. "We'll have to do something to celebrate."

"That's what Father John told me last year, too." I sighed. It still hurt, even after six months. Father John had been the first person I remembered after my fall. When I was released from the hospital after my abrupt arrival in a local park, he had taken me in and let me live at the church and taught me almost everything I knew of the world. He'd died the following autumn, murdered by a demon for trying to make the city a better place. Or at least that's what we assumed. The demon hadn't exactly been forthcoming with its evil plot. Unlike in the movies, demons don't typically monologue. They might have the ego of a comic book villain, but they're usually intelligent enough to play their cards close to the chest.

Jim put a hand on my shoulder, squeezing firmly. "He was right. You, me, Dust, and Eirlas will have to get together and do something fun. Hopefully by then, we'll have your housing situation figured out." He sighed. "You not having ID makes all of this much more complicated, but we'll find a way."

He was right, of course. I had no form of identification whatsoever since I hadn't even been born on the *planet*, let alone in the country. As such, I had no way of obtaining any sort of documentation, which made my situation in Boston somewhat tenuous and limited the places I could find work. Or so Eirlas had told me. Of the three of them, he knew the most about that system since he dealt with people who didn't have ID all the time at the shelter. It also meant I couldn't rent an apartment, get any sort of assistance with my housing or food situation, or most of the other safety net programs.

It frustrated me because I was willing to work—I wanted to work—but some foolish paperwork and nonsense stood in the way. I couldn't conceive of the notion of a slip of paper making such a difference, but Eirlas had told me being undocumented changed things for me. Until we figured out how to acquire me identification, I was stuck in a perpetual limbo. Yet another facet of life that made me want to grind my teeth. It's a wonder I have any left.

"We will..." I stopped and took a breath. "*We'll* figure it out."

Jim gave me an encouraging smile as he navigated the slushy streets. "Good catch." He took us through a McDonald's drive-thru and bought both of us dinner on the way toward his apartment building.

We parked in his usual place and ate in comfortable silence before I zipped up my jacket again, not looking forward to the long, dark hours of freezing temperatures that awaited me outside. The temperature had dropped from just above freezing to well below when the sun had gone down several hours ago. "Thank you, Jim."

"Of course, Cass. You're family." For all he smiled, guilt lingered in his eyes. It wasn't his fault, but no matter how many times I told him that, he still took it personally for some reason.

I suspected my banishment was because Father Demoyne and I had several loud arguments about theology when he made statements about the Father's will that were categorically wrong. Father Demoyne didn't appreciate being told he was wrong. Most people don't, but given his position as a priest, I couldn't stand by and let him teach mistranslations and errors as literal gospel. No matter how many times Jim tried to tell me not to fight with him about it.

On the other hand, whenever I did get into one of those fights, Jim and Dust seemed to enjoy me dressing him down. More than once, Dust had commented to Jim that they should keep popcorn on hand. Jim had scolded him, but he'd been laughing, so it didn't quite stick.

Were it not for the fact that St. Mary's was home, I would have gone elsewhere, but I couldn't bring myself to leave it. Not after everything that happened there and the memories I had of Father John. I still could almost feel the gentle old priest in the quiet places around the church when nobody else was around. Even hear his voice as he patiently taught me how to negotiate things like chores, interpersonal interactions, and just life in general. It hurt, but that connection was one of the reasons I couldn't bear to leave the place. That, and I had pleasant associations with a number of the homeless folk the shelter and soup kitchen served.

"Good night," I said, smiling back at Jim before I went to climb out of the car.

Jim stopped me with a hand on my arm. "Do you have everything you need? Blankets, socks, hand warmers..." He trailed off, his brows furrowed.

I put my hand over his and squeezed, maintaining my smile as I looked into his sad brown eyes. "I'm all right, Jim. If I need anything, I will tell you. I have my phone, and I will call."

He looked like he wanted to say something but instead nodded once, a sharp jerk of his chin that seemed more for himself than me in some ways. "Good. You'd better." His tone was a little gruff, which usually meant he was trying to control his emotions.

I released his hand and stepped out of the car into the evening gloom.

# CHAPTER 2

I walked down Mass. Ave. toward the bridge, leaving footprints in the heavy slush on the ground. We'd had snow recently, but it hadn't stayed the lovely white it had been when it first fell. What remained was a "cold, wet bucket of suck," as Dust deemed it. Despite wearing two pairs of socks, my feet chilled as the slush seeped into my shoes. I had dry socks at camp and looked forward to changing them. Of all the things I'd learned in my time being homeless, an appreciation for dry clothing had been one of the chief lessons I had gained.

Hugging the right side of the bridge, I took the pedestrian ramp down, careful not to slip on the icy, freezing awfulness that coated the descent. Halfway to ground level, I leaned on the railing and looked out across the Charles River. While living on the street had drawbacks, I never stopped enjoying the beauty of the water. I imagined living here might be more tolerable — or even pleasant — in the summer with the breeze coming off it to cool the heavy, humid air in the warmer months.

I stood there for a few minutes, watching the lights of Cambridge reflecting on the river's surface and considering my life. Certainly, I didn't enjoy some aspects of living on Earth, but others I was glad of. Since my fall from Heaven, I had learned a lot and understood far more about the Father's world than I ever had as a gate guardian. Even if I did sometimes miss the solitude and quiet. This world was so bright and loud, and it moved so quickly, I often had no idea what to do with myself.

The days had started to blur together when I had fallen into a routine of living here under the bridge and working at the church. The weather changed, the seasons shifted, but most days, it was the same. There was some measure of comfort in that since, before my fall, time hadn't been relevant to me whatsoever. The repetition felt safe and familiar in a way. At the same time, however, the knowledge there was some purpose for me that I had yet to fulfill tugged at the edges of my consciousness.

The previous autumn, just after my fight with the demon responsible for Father John's death, I had learned I wasn't entirely forgotten down here. The angel assigned to watch me — a malak named Codiel — had told me there was a plan for me. A fraction of my former power had been returned with the intent that I would use it to fulfill the purpose I had been given. Of course, I had no idea what my purpose was. So, more or less, I had been stuck in a holding pattern until I learned more or something in my situation changed. I tried to rely on faith, but that can be hard to do when you don't know where your next meal is coming from or whether or not you'll freeze to death in your sleep. Even for those of us who know with absolute certainty that there is a divine plan. After all, sometimes things happen that make no sense, like priests being murdered by demons, people dying in plagues and wars, and other such atrocities. It's beyond the scope of my comprehension and always has been, but it's not for me to understand. But that doesn't make it easier.

I hadn't told Jim or the others about Codiel or his statement of my purpose yet. While they had been willing to help me handle the whole mess, I knew how terrified they had been when facing down real demons. And until I knew more, I didn't want to frighten them. Besides, if I was going to be dealing with demons, I didn't want to drag them into it if I could avoid it.

My breath hung in the air in front of me as I sighed. I knew I had to wait. I would be told what I needed to know when I needed it, but that didn't make being patient any easier.

Pulling away from the railing, I continued down the ramp to the foot path that ran along the edge of the river and jogged across Storrow Drive between cars to reach the spot where the camp huddled underneath the girders of the bridge.

There were maybe ten of us tucked in there, using the bridge to keep the weather off of us. The others had said it was a short-term solution since the police regularly came through and drove people off, but I had been here most nights for the past month and had been left alone so far. Having been taught to draw as little attention as possible, I limited my comings and goings to well after dark or before dawn when it was easiest to slip in and out without being caught.

Ether, the woman who more or less led the small group, looked in my direction when I ducked into the space, her eyes reflecting the light like a cat's. I had learned early on that she was a vampire, though she'd been quick to reassure me that she wasn't going to do me harm. Not that I had been afraid. She was a little shorter than my six feet but much thinner with sallow skin and very deep-set eyes. From what I understood of vampires, that meant she had been unwell before she had been turned, since once turned, vampires didn't age or really show much for outward displays of sickness or health.

Father Demoyne claimed vampires were Satan's children, trying to subvert the Father's will by avoiding death. Yet another one of our arguments since whether they died sooner or later, all things eventually pass, no matter how old. Even immortals like vampires and fae can die by means other than aging. And elves, I had reminded him, lived hundreds upon hundreds of years. He had sputtered and glowered at me when I brought up his heritage and claimed that it wasn't the point, and he'd flounced off shortly thereafter.

"Hey, Cass," Ether said with a crooked half-smile that revealed one of her fangs. She and a couple of the others were huddled around a tiny little fire in a clear area of the encampment. Maggie, another regular, was a mage and often used magic to help keep us warm and dry as best she could. She was how I'd found this place.

Maggie was also a regular at St. Mary's, and I'd grown to know her over the last few months when she'd started coming in. I didn't know her story or why she was homeless, but it always struck me that it must have been something to do with her family. She regularly talked about her time in college at Harvard but avoided conversation about anything that led her here. The pain in her eyes and the way she had adopted the rest of us as family so quickly spoke to the deep loneliness I guessed she felt.

I sunk down near the fire and put my feet near it, letting the hot little flame melt the slush on my shoes. "Hello Ether, Maggie." I nodded to both of them. "How are you today?"

They, and the others in the camp, had accepted my strange speech patterns without hesitation. They didn't mind that I rarely used contractions or sometimes struggled with words. When I didn't understand some simple facet of the world, they didn't judge. Instead, they taught me what I needed to know. A stark contrast to the way a number of the more affluent members of the church treated me. The poor and lost had always been more accepting of my oddities. Maybe because so many of them had oddities of their own.

"Doing okay," Ether answered with a noncommittal shrug. "Haven't seen Chester today, but he'll turn up. He always does."

"I think he said he was going to the VA to raise hell about getting more insulin." Maggie spoke up, glancing at the two of us. "I got a job interview today."

I grinned at her. "Congratulations. I a—" I paused and sighed. "I'm happy for you," I said, correcting myself.

"Thanks, Cass. How'd your meeting go?"

Ether made a face when Maggie mentioned the church. She hated religion. After having seen the way Father Demoyne thought of and treated her kind, I couldn't blame her. "I'll never understand why you keep going there."

Unlike with Father Demoyne, Ether's dislike for my faith made sense to me, and more than that, I hurt for her. To be that angry, she had to have been treated terribly. A feeling I understood. I had learned with unfortunate clarity that churches were so often not what they were supposed to be. "Because it's how I help people. The kitchen serves anyone who needs food, Christian or not. And it's where my friends are." I shrugged. "It went all right."

"Yeah, they supposedly help the needy and let you volunteer there but won't let you stay? It's bullshit, Cass, and you know it. They're happy to take advantage of your willingness to help, but do they give anything in return?"

I sighed, lowering my eyes. A pang of loss made my heart feel like it was missing a beat for a moment before I spoke again. "Father John did. And Jim is the best friend anyone could ask for. He does his best."

Something in the tone of my voice shut Ether up, and she dropped the subject. For all her sharp manner, she had a good heart. When I'd first come here, it had been Ether who'd made sure I had a space to sleep. She'd shown me how to layer cardboard over the ground to help keep me off the chill earth. She'd checked in on me to make sure I knew how to get in and out of here without being seen, and she made sure all of the people in our little group had what they needed to the best of her ability. Also, she didn't feed on the people she camped with. I didn't know where she got what she needed, but it seemed rude to ask.

Maggie, ever the cheerful one, bulldozed on ahead, ignoring the tension. "I'm glad. Jim's a good guy. I've always liked him."

"Where did you go for your interview?" I asked, glad to get off the topic of St. Mary's.

"Oh. Just a Starbucks. Eirlas is letting me use the address of the shelter to put down for job recommendations." Maggie smiled.

I smiled back. "That's great news." The words were honest, but I would be lying if I didn't admit a certain pang of jealousy.

Maggie nodded. "Yeah, it's been a big help. He also makes sure I get my mail if anything shows up there. He's great."

That sounded like the Eirlas I knew. He went out of his way to do everything he could for people on the street because he'd been one of us not too many years ago. His former life, before prison, he'd been in a gang and deeply involved in the drug trade. He didn't like to talk about those years and shied away from the topic whenever it came up. "He is," I agreed.

It was then that I felt the Blight.

# CHAPTER 3

As a fallen angel, I retained some remnants of my Grace, the power of creation through which all things came to be. Grace is also what makes up the soul. Everything from humans to cypress trees has a bit of Grace in it, albeit to differing degrees and volumes. Conversely, demons have a twisted version of that power known as Blight. While neither of these is the exact word for them in Enochian, it's as close as I can get in this language, and it's the term those in the know understand.

Feeling Blight from nearby, all thoughts of changing my socks and sleep fled my mind, and I looked around, trying to pinpoint its location. "I'll be back," I said by way of explanation and rose from near the fire, slipping out between the bridge's supports. I could feel Maggie and Ether's eyes on me as I left, but neither of them tried to stop me.

It took me a few moments to locate where the Blight was strongest, but the feeling was moving above me down Mass. Ave. The demon must be crossing the bridge.

Not for the first time, I wished I had some kind of weapon. Checking to make sure there was nobody adjacent, I summoned my wings, which burst out of the wing slits on my jacket. I then jogged up the embankment, intending to use the slope as a taking off point. I could get airborne from a standstill if I had to, but it was harder than one may imagine.

At the top of the embankment, I looked around again and spotted a figure wearing a long coat walking down the sidewalk toward Cambridge. Blight poured off him like smoke and pooled around his footprints as he passed. I couldn't make much out from that distance, but I caught the air and flew across the space separating us, landing in the slush a good ten feet away.

If the demon noticed me, he made no indication of it, and I took the opportunity to close on it. "What are you doing here, demon?" I spat the words, preparing to fight.

When the figure turned to face me, his face registered first surprise and then amusement. "Well hello there." Under the long coat, the man wore the most expensive suit I'd ever seen. Waistcoat and everything, all in a dark color I couldn't make out in the evening gloom. His smile was easy, though the burning coal red of his eyes gave him away. As did the heavy sense of Blight he wore like a mantle. His face was handsome in the ethereal, unnatural way of celestial creatures, his pale skin was similar to mine, and his features were similar enough that he was either good at faking or had, perhaps, been an angel himself once. His hair was dark enough that I couldn't tell the color at night, but he had it short and impeccably groomed, much like the rest of him. "I wasn't expecting to see you out here."

I grit my teeth. "Answer the question."

"So testy." He lifted his hands, smile never faltering. "I'm not here for you, don't worry."

"That does not make it better." I took a step forward, fire igniting around my hands and sliding up my forearms. While holy fire looks more or less like real fire, it isn't, and it doesn't catch physical objects unless I really put effort into it. My holy fire manifests in a blue the same shade as my eyes. After the events at the drug lab earlier in the year, the blue had returned, and I suspected it was tied to the partial renewal of my Grace. The flames wavered and flickered, casting stark, hard shadows on the ground around us as they licked up my skin.

In retrospect, getting up in a demon's face like that wasn't the smartest thing I've ever done.

He squinted against the light, eyes averting. "I'm looking for something. Once I find it, I'm gone. Don't worry your sweet little head."

I glowered at him, the endearments making me want to punch him. "What are you looking for?"

"Oh, angel, that would be telling, wouldn't it? Besides, would you believe I'm trying to help?"

"No."

"Well, there you have it. Now, if you'll excuse me, I have business to tend to." He bowed his head politely and took a step away before turning his back to me and striding down the sidewalk in the direction he'd been going.

I lowered my hands and considered for a moment before starting after him.

The demon spun toward me again as if he felt me following him, his movement so sudden and swift that I almost walked into him. I had to stop so short, I overbalanced and stumbled. Ow. My dignity.

"No, no. This is not for you. Stay out of it." His tone was sharp, and he was no longer smiling. Instead, he looked almost concerned. "I suggest you find some other way of entertaining yourself. Surely, there are other things for you to do in the city. Other battles to fight."

My mouth tugged downward into a scowl. "As if that is genuine. Your kind does not worry for mine." I grabbed his shirt and dragged him close to me. He was hot to the touch even through the fabric of his clothes. It would have been pleasant if it weren't from such an odious source. "You *will* tell me what this is about, or I will smite you." I didn't know if I could back that up, but since he hadn't shown any inclination toward wanting to fight me just yet, I decided to take the risk.

The holy fire still wreathed around my hands must have singed him because he hissed through his teeth, trying to pull away despite my hold on his clothing. "As you wish." His tone was tight and raw, leaning his head away from the flames. "Since you asked *so* nicely, I will tell you. But only once you've released me. You are ruffling my shirt."

All of that, and he was worried about his shirt. I released him. "Do not make me regret this."

He stepped away, brushing himself off, expression indignant. "Spicy little thing, aren't you? Since you insist on shoving your nose in, you may be of some use to me. I'm after one of the nails. It's believed to be here in this city, and a group of demons is after it. I intend to stop them."

I narrowed my eyes at him. "Now was that so hard?"

"Yes, actually. It was. Now, if you would kindly leave me, I have business to tend to, plots to hatch, schemes to create, and trouble to cause." His mouth twisted, expression showing deep displeasure as he finished righting his clothing. I must have hurt him with holy fire that close, but he didn't comment on it.

My worries that he was more powerful than I could easily deal with on my own confirmed, I nodded once. It confused me that he'd been so forthcoming, which led me to think this was probably a trap of some kind. But even if it was, if one of the nails *was* in the city, and demons *were* after it, there was real trouble coming.

The nails he must've referred to were the nails that had held Jesus to the cross. There were three of them — one for each hand, one for His feet. While they were usually referred to as "nails," they were closer to the size of railroad spikes. And they were some of the most powerful holy relics on Earth. There were, of course, many relics in the world, but few had the raw potential of the nails. Only one other surpassed them: the crown of thorns.

While I stood there chewing over the new information, the demon turned away from me again and continued in the direction he'd been going without further comment. I let him go, watching his back as he walked down the length of the bridge until I lost the outline of him in the shadow between two street lights. What did this mean? Of course, all of this could have been a ruse of some kind. He had no reason to tell me the truth, and the idea of a demon being honest was, quite honestly, laughable.

So I did the only thing I could think of: I prayed.

Last autumn, when I had lain dying and damaged in a drug lab after my fight with the demon responsible for the enterprise, one of my siblings had come to tell me he was my watcher. In that time, he'd mentioned that if I called out to him, he would hear. Which was what I did now.

It didn't take long for him to answer, which surprised me. In retrospect, it shouldn't have, given that his duty was to watch me. But at the time, I was startled when he appeared off to my left in the street in the same white robe I had seen him wear the last time he had visited.

Codiel is, as all angels are, supernaturally beautiful. Elves might be the most beautiful creatures on Earth, but angels outstrip them in spades. Well, the ones who resemble anything remotely human, anyhow. Most of us wear human guises when interacting with the world, however. Were we to reveal our true nature to those around us, most would descend into gibbering insanity. Something about wheels with eyes. Mortal minds cannot comprehend us well, which produces *interesting* results. While Codiel and I are different choirs of angel, we have some similar features: our eyes, the shape of our jaw, our nose. Most people who have ever seen us together can tell we are related. Insomuch as we truly are.

While angels call each other brother, sister, or sibling, we aren't related in the mortal sense — after all, we are not born of mortal parents and do not breed the way creatures on Earth do unless we are fallen. It's more like we are from a similar mold. Most angels of the same choir bear a strong resemblance to one another, almost to the point of being indistinguishable beyond our hair, eye, and wing color. Even the similarity between choirs is still quite notable. Between Codiel and I, my hair is dark and cut very short, and my wings are ashen gray, while his hair is a golden blonde, and his wings are a similar shade. Both of us have a similar shade of exceptionally blue eyes, though, like a brilliant summer sky. Mine are darker than Codiel's, but unless you see the two of us standing adjacent, it's hard to tell.

On instinct, I grabbed a handful of his perfect white robe and yanked him over to the sidewalk.

Codiel's face bore the most utterly confused expression I'd ever seen on any creature, and that made me laugh a little. Though the confusion swiftly turned to mild offense. "*What was that for?*" he asked in Enochian, his tone somewhere between scolding and curious.

"*You should not stand in the street,*" I explained, slipping into the familiarity of the language I knew best. It sounded rather silly since, as an angel, the likelihood of him being hit by a car was, well, low. But I'd learned quickly that getting in the way of one was a terrible idea after I'd seen a possessed man leap into traffic.

"*…Right. What was it you needed, Cassiel?*" He sighed, obviously a little annoyed at being dragged around by his robes. He adjusted them with a bit of obvious dismay at how I'd rumpled the fabric.

"Was what that demon told me true? Is one of the nails here in Boston?"

Codiel was silent for a long time as though trying to figure out what to tell me and how to tell it. The conflict on his face told me more than his words likely would. "*I cannot give you that information, exactly. But I can tell you there are things afoot that are tied to your purpose,*" he drawled. "*If such a thing like that were in the city, surely demons would be looking for it. And if they were looking for it, surely they would intend to do something terrible with that kind of power.*"

I could tell he was walking a line and had more or less told me without telling me that the demon had been right. Defying the spirit of his edict even if he wasn't defying the details was dicey at best, though, so I didn't press him for details. "*I see,*" I said, leaning against the rail that separated us from the drop down onto Storrow Drive beneath.

Storrow Drive is one of the arterial roads in Boston, and even at night, it has a steady flow of cars moving along it, though that tends to quiet down after the bars close at two in the morning. The hum and splash of tires and engines beneath us filled the silence.

Codiel lingered, looking like he wanted to say more but at the same time offering nothing. Instead, he just watched the city.

When the quiet became awkward, I sighed. *"So he was telling the truth,"* I said more to myself than to Codiel.

"I cannot say whether he was or not."

"I wasn't really asking," I replied, shaking my head. "I am not asking you to break your mandate. Thank you, brother."

He bowed his head, golden hair falling in his face. *"You are welcome, sister. I am sorry I am not more help."* His tone suggested genuine regret. Not that he would have lied about it, of course, but the apology sounded honest and troubled. *"I should go."*

I nodded. "Go with God, brother."

And then he was gone, like someone blowing out a candle, leaving me alone on the bridge.

# CHAPTER 4

I made my way down off the bridge and back under it, slipping between the supports and into the enclosed space where we stayed. Ether fixed me with a long look. "Everything okay?" she asked, tone a little worried.

"Yes, sorry. I…" I fished for an answer. "I had to make a phone call." While it wasn't really true, I had called out to Codiel, though I disliked lying.

Ether raised a brow. "You're a terrible liar. If you don't want to explain something, don't. But you don't need to lie." She shook her head.

"Sorry." I sighed. Maggie was lying down in her usual spot by then, burrowed into her sleeping bag. The idea appealed, and I realized I still hadn't changed my socks. My feet were extremely cold. "I don't want to discuss it." I made my way over to my spot and sat down, pulling off my drenched shoes and socks and putting on a dry pair, saying a silent thanks to Jim for constantly making sure I had them. He'd given me a few packs of good wool socks to distribute to the others as well. We had all benefited from his kindness.

"All right. Just… you don't look so good. If something's going down, you know the people here will have your back, right?"

I didn't want to have to tell her their help wasn't likely to be much given the circumstances, but I nodded. The intent mattered even if they weren't exactly demon hunters. "I know, and I appreciate it."

Ether stood and stretched, putting out Maggie's little fire. "I have to go find food. Just wanted to make sure you got in okay."

"I'm all right." I gave her a tired half-smile in the darkness. I knew she'd see it.

She left the camp, and I crawled into my sleeping bag, burying myself in it with my jeans, shirt, and jacket still on. Every layer mattered in winter. Cushioning my head on my arm, I stared into the darkness while listening to the sounds of passing cars. The sound had become my lullaby over the last few months, and it helped soothe the stress boiling under my skin.

The demon had been honest about what was going on, but what his angle was, I didn't know. Why tell me anything, much less the truth? Of course, I could be ascribing more forethought than he was really giving it, but I found it better to expect a demon to be more conniving than not. Particularly the more powerful ones.

An archdemon, which was what I suspected he was, was a demon who had once been an angel. Unlike me, they had not merely fallen from grace, they had joined the ranks of Hell for whatever reason.

The various choirs and types of angels have differing power and skills. I am a seraph and an angel of battle, for example. Codiel is a malak (the plural being malakim) and serves as a messenger or scribe. I won't bore you with Heaven's entire power structure. I'm not sure it's yours to know anyway, but the only class of angel with more raw power than a seraph—which is what I am—is an archangel. They are the heads of entire divisions, and humanity knows most of them by name: Michael, Raphael, Gabriel, Uriel, and so on. Malakim are the rank and file angels, and there are more of them than there are of any of the others.

The problem with my new "friend" being an archdemon was I had no idea what or who he had been before his fall, so I couldn't predict his possible power level. If what little I'd felt around him was any indication, though, he was certainly more potent than a malak. I'd faced an archdemon once before, but I knew I'd been lucky more than anything. I'd thrown myself at it in a suicidal attempt to destroy the thing, and I'd succeeded. I credit my victory more to the forces of Heaven than I do myself since, without some form of intercession on their part, I would have died in that warehouse.

My fall from Heaven had happened because I'd made a mistake and trusted a demon. I was in no ready mood to make such a mistake a second time.

I rolled onto my back and sighed, draping my arm over my eyes. Whatever was happening, whatever this was about, I needed sleep. That had to come first. I'd talk to Jim about it tomorrow evening when I saw him. Besides, he might have an idea of how to track down a holy relic in the city. Codiel had told me, without telling me, that the nail was here, and the threat was real. Which meant I needed to track it down before the demons could get their claws on it.

As if I had any idea how.

---

Eventually, I fell into a restless sleep, dreaming of my fall, of the fight in the drug lab, of shadowed figures lurking just outside the edges of my vision. When I woke, I did so with a start. I'd felt like I was falling, and the impact woke me, though I hadn't moved from where I'd dozed off. Though I had, I realized, fallen asleep with a rock under me that had spent the night jabbing into my back, leaving the muscles stiff and angry.

I sat up, pulling my pay-as-you-go phone out of my pocket and checking the time. It was only six AM. I'd slept about the expected eight hours, and it was still dark outside. Well, insomuch as it ever was in the city.

I squirmed out of my sleeping bag and opened it up to shake out any dust or debris that had been on my clothes when I'd climbed into it. I couldn't really keep it clean what with me sleeping on a few pieces of cardboard on the ground, but I did my best. Maggie was still curled up in her own nest of sleeping bag and a few blankets she'd salvaged, and a few other similar lumps lay on the ground around me.

After cleaning things up, I got my toothbrush, toothpaste, deodorant, soap, and water bottle from my backpack and crept off to the side to clean up for the day. It didn't take me long, but it was little things like that, that helped keep me together. And a luxury I knew many in my position didn't have. Eirlas and Jim had been adamant about ensuring I had toiletries. When I finished, I put my things in my backpack, pausing to pick up the prescription pill bottle that held the cocktail umbrella Father John had given me. It had survived my pocket and the events of my life for the last year until Jim had finally suggested I put it in something more protective.

The umbrella itself was nothing special: just a red-and-yellow cocktail umbrella from a bar. The paper was a bit ratty and scuffed, and part of the end of the toothpick had snapped off. Honestly, it was nothing to look at, but I treasured it more than anything else in my possession. It had been part of the last conversation I'd had with Father

John before he'd been murdered. After too many pints of Guinness, he'd bought me a fruity drink with the umbrella in it and had laughed when I tried to wrap my head around its purpose.

He'd asked me that night what good angels were since none of us had been there to save his sister and nephew from the demon that had killed them. I hadn't known how to answer. While I couldn't do anything about the past, I had resolved to make a difference now and in the future. It was the best honor I could do to his memory.

Knowing it really didn't make a difference, I slid the pill bottle into my jacket pocket as though it would bring me good luck. Or bring me closer to him. I doubted it would do either, but it made me feel marginally better, which helped. The weather today had turned rainy, and I sighed, not looking forward to battling the moisture on top of the cold. At least it wasn't below freezing that I could tell. Small mercies.

I fished a pair of plastic shopping bags out of my backpack and put them over my socks before donning my shoes. I then tucked the plastic up into my pantlegs. It wasn't too obvious, I decided, and it was one of the various techniques I'd learned to help keep my feet dry and as warm as possible. This time of year, keeping my feet dry and warm was more important than I could have imagined, but I'd learned quickly why socks were always in such high demand at the shelter.

Ready for the day, I folded up my sleeping bag and set my backpack on it. We had an agreement, those who lived here, that we didn't touch each other's things, and for the most part, everyone adhered to that. I didn't have anything of value anyway, so if someone did steal my personal possessions, they'd only have gotten my few toiletries, a change of clothes, and a Bible out of the effort. And if somebody needed those things badly enough to steal them from me, they could have them. I was lucky enough to be able to replace them if it came to it, even if it would be a chore and some measure of frustration.

I left the shelter of the bridge and headed south, into the city. I had a couple of hours before Jim would be awake, and I didn't really want to disturb him. Besides, I'd see him later that day when we went over to the shelter. However, I did walk by his building and glance at his windows to make sure everything looked all right. Maybe it was paranoia after seeing the demon, but I'd wanted to make sure he was safe.

Everything looked normal for this time of day, so I continued wandering, following Mass. Ave. with no real direction in mind.

It was a familiar thing these days since I didn't have much to do unless I was at the church. I'd initially tried to find work, but when I couldn't produce an ID, nobody I'd met had been willing to hire me. That left me with a great deal of time on my hands. The upside of all of this, however, was I'd grown to know the five-mile stretch between where Jim lived and the church relatively well.

Today found me making the forty-five minute walk to Franklin Park. It wasn't much for shelter from the rain, but it was pretty, and nobody told me to move along while I was walking around the place so long as I didn't draw too much attention. In winter, the zoo and golf course were closed, which also meant I more or less had the space to myself. I hoped it would help me think.

By the time I reached the park, the sun had crested the horizon. I found a bench out of the way and sat down, resting my elbows on my knees as I took slow, measured breaths of the cold, moist air. Jim and Eirlas had talked to me a lot about working through anxiety, and I had become adept at grounding whenever I felt it starting to swallow me. That demon the night before, the idea of one of the nails being in the city, all of that had my chest feeling tight. If Codiel was right, and I was supposed to deal with this, my first step had to be finding the nail.

But then what?

I deeply doubted I could just walk in and say, *"Hi, angel of the Lord here, can I have that? Thanks!"* And even if I did take it, what would I do with it? How would I keep it safe? Could I even keep it safe? I had no idea.

My hands trembled, and I looked down at them, splaying my fingers.

I have broad hands with long fingers. More than once, people in my life have suggested I play piano. Though to me, they always look more like a warrior's hands than a musician's. I've never been any good with instruments. I can sing, of course—all angels can—but instruments have never spoken to me that way. My palms and fingers are calloused from wielding a sword and shield since time immemorial, and that roughness will never fade.

My skin was pale from the cold, I noticed. I didn't really feel it, but my fingers weren't numb. Jim had warned me about frostbite many times, so I knew the signs to look for. At least I had that. I closed my eyes, focusing on my breathing. *A plan, Cassiel. Put together a plan.*

I didn't notice them until it was too late.

# CHAPTER 5

A sharp pain tore into my right shoulder and bicep. I jumped up off the bench, turning toward the source of the sensation just in time for a second attack to rake across my shoulders. While it hurt, I was honestly more angry about the destruction of my coat. A group of demons wearing the guise of teenagers surrounded me, just out of arm's reach. I recognized them for what they were regardless of the ruse. Despite wearing the correct clothes and adopting the correct posture, the shadowy, indistinct blur of their faces gave them away. As did the feel of their Blight.

I counted five or six of them in front of me, but the feeling of Blight behind me told me there were more behind.

Summoning holy fire to my fingertips, I leaned to the side as one of them lunged at me. I grabbed one of the attacker's outstretched arms and hurled it into the demon behind me. It screamed as the fire around my hands touched it, though I hadn't called enough to smite the thing entirely. While I could fight, and fight well, life is not an action movie, and one person against six in close quarters like I was, is not a recipe for success. However this ended, it was going to hurt.

They moved in all at once, lashing out at me with their claws, tearing at whatever of me they could reach. I had no idea what they wanted—if anything—beyond the relentless savagery of destruction, but I didn't have time to ask. Instead, I manifested my wings and snapped them open, hurling several away and creating an opening in the fight to either side.

I feinted left and dove to the right, over one of the demons I had knocked prone with a wing. I hit the ground in a roll and came up on my feet, running down the pathway deeper into the park.

I am not built for speed. Not like a sprinter, anyway. I've always been more of a plant-my-feet-and-fight kind of combatant, given that I was created to guard a gate. But what I lack in speed, I make up for with endurance.

In this case, I wasn't trying to outrun my pursuers. More just draw them with me so I could choose a place to make my stand. They snarled and slavered behind me as they gave chase. With the amount of blood I could feel pouring down my skin under my ruined jacket and shirt, I knew I only had so long before I got lightheaded and would need to stop. Adrenaline would only get me so far, and they'd lain me open deep in some places.

"This way." I recognized the voice and glanced into the trees to see the archdemon I'd met the night before gesturing to me.

I threw a handful of holy flame in his direction and kept running, my lip curling into a snarl.

He made an annoyed noise. "There's a spot back there where you can make a stand."

"As if I would trust you," I snapped, pushing myself faster.

The archdemon kept pace with me by appearing and disappearing every few yards, leaning against another tree with an indolent, if somewhat annoyed, expression. "With the amount of blood you're losing, you don't have a choice. Either go and make your stand, or stay out in the open and get torn apart. It's an old part of the zoo near here. You can funnel them in to you."

"Why help me?"

"I'm bored."

I slowed to a stop, panting. He was right about the blood loss. I was beginning to shiver from shock, and I didn't have much time before I'd reach the end of my rope. Gritting my teeth, I studied him. The suit he had on was different somehow than the other one, but I couldn't put my finger on it. A slightly different color? A different tie? The details didn't really register. "Fine. Where?" I knew this was probably a trap so he could kill me. Or worse. But I was out of options, and if I didn't find a tactical advantage soon, they'd kill me pretty quickly.

"Oh, so *now* you listen. Follow me." He smirked and turned off the path into the trees.

I followed, hearing the pack of demons behind me growing closer. Time started developing the strange, liquid feeling I always got when I was hurt and in shock. Everything felt slower, and I fumbled my way after the archdemon.

Not far from where he'd gestured to me the first time was exactly what he'd said: the ruins of an old zoo exhibit sat nearby. The ten-foot fences of rusted steel had a single doorway leading into a concrete enclosure. It wasn't perfect, but at least I had a better chance of controlling the space than I had before. A large relief nearby displayed a pair of bears, but the weather had worn away most of the writing, leaving only a date below it: 1912.

I registered the details as part of my tactical assessment, though it all felt a little foggy. I stumbled as I turned to face the doorway, my back to the wall.

The archdemon put his hand on my shoulder to steady me, the heat I'd felt the night before pouring into me through my coat. "You're no good like this," he grumbled, looking me over. He didn't have a chance to finish whatever thought he was trying to convey before the others caught up. Instead of turning on me, however, he put himself between me and them, holding out his hands. "The angel is mine, hell spawn. Go find other prey."

They hesitated long enough that I guessed I'd been right about the level of threat the archdemon presented. However, the pause gave way to them lunging forward to try and get around him to reach me. No matter how quick he was, there were more of them than there were of us. While skill, power, and training can overcome a lot, there's much to be said for sheer numbers.

I'd risked trusting him this far, so I grit my teeth and grabbed the archdemon by the back of the shirt. I yanked him toward me, putting us both to the wall. At least they couldn't get behind us. He shot me a look and nodded once in a moment of complete understanding before the chaos started.

Pouring Grace into my hands, I felt my lips curl up into a feral grimace of fury as I lunged at the first demon to come in arm's reach. Instead of just grabbing it as I had before, however, I forced my power through it.

The creature screamed and turned to ash in my hands.

I could only do it so many times without destroying myself, but this was a good test of the renewed connection to my Grace Codiel told me I possessed. I figured fighting for my life against a pack of demons counted as using it for the power of good, so I was probably safe.

After I wrecked the first of them, the second jumped on me from the side. It stuck claws into my already-torn shoulder and back, trying to stay out of the way of my hands. As if that were the only way I could channel holy fire. The pain felt distant now, which I knew wasn't a good sign, but I'd had worse. After nearly burning to death and being torn to shreds last autumn, this was nothing. Well, maybe not nothing, but certainly far less worrisome.

Flame erupted from the demon where it contacted me, and it let go with a screech, falling back and away. I used the opportunity to grab it by its strange not-a-face and finish the job. That was two.

The third I caught trying to get between me and the archdemon to flank him. It made the poor choice of putting its back to me, so I took advantage of that, leaving it a smoking pile of ashes at my feet.

I finished just in time to see my strange companion driving a wicked-looking knife into the last of his share of our adversaries. Whatever had happened to the other two, I couldn't say, but the last demon froze, a grimace on its face, and collapsed inward on itself, becoming dust, and the dust fading to nothing.

A long moment of tension hung between myself and the suited archdemon while I waited to see if he was going to turn that knife on me. Instead, he wiped it off on his sleeve and tucked it into his jacket. He extended a hand to me, stepping in close enough that I could feel the heat of him. His hand touched my shoulder. "Sit, dear angel." He gestured to a large rock in the enclosure. "You look positively abysmal."

Staggering over, I sunk onto the rock, trying to find my focus as everything blurred and swam.

He had followed me, I realized. "We should get you help," he said, his handsome features set in a frown. "You're a disaster."

Something about the way he phrased that amused me, and I chuckled, though I caught myself before it became the manic cackle that threatened. This was an archdemon. A manifestation of evil. If he was being friendly, he had a plan. "Why?"

"Because you've bled all over your clothing and are pale as a cloud."

"No. Why help?"

The demon sighed. "I told you, I was bored."

"Not good enough."

"Tough." A self-satisfied grin curled his lips. "I don't answer to you." He looked me over and shook his head. "I shall return. I'd say don't go anywhere, but…" He waved a vague hand indicating my condition. Then he vanished in a faint puff of sulfur-scented smoke.

# CHAPTER 6

I sat alone in the bear enclosure for a few minutes, cold, dizzy, and hurting. Part of me thought it might be a good idea to call Jim. He had EMT training and would've helped me in a heartbeat. But the idea of pulling my phone out of my pocket and dialing the number exhausted me. Instead, I rested my elbows on my knees, banished my wings again, and tried to take stock of everything.

My back, shoulders, and outside of my arms had the worst of it, I guessed. Taking off the ruined jacket and shirt would've been hard to do on my own, so I couldn't see for sure, but the cold ache of deep wounds had spread across those areas of my body pretty clearly. While there was pain, the worst part of it was the foreign, awful feeling of air and rain in places they shouldn't touch. If you've never had a wound like that, the sensation is almost impossible to describe, but the sense of *wrongness* is worse. At least to me.

"Here we are," the archdemon said, his voice coming from my right as he popped into being next to me. "Now, dear angel, this is going to hurt, but since the alternative is bleeding to death, I don't imagine you'll argue."

I blinked a few times, trying to focus again as I turned my head toward him. "Huh?"

He sighed, walking around in front of me and crouching. "Look at me, angel."

"Name's Cass," I said, annoyed that my voice slurred. But I looked at him.

"I'm going to cauterize the worst of these or you *will* bleed to death. You don't like me or trust me. I understand that. You're right not to, but we don't have alternatives right now. I'm going to help you out of what's left of your clothes, stop the bleeding, and get you into new clothes. Do you understand?"

I understood. Mostly. I wanted to reject his help and tell him to get lost, but I just didn't have the energy.

He watched my eyes for a moment, looking for something. Whether he saw it or not, I didn't know. Standing, he donned a pair of blue nitrile gloves before stripping me out of my jacket and shirt with surprising efficiency. He was gentle about it, but that didn't make it hurt much less, and white spots exploded across my vision as he moved me. I hissed in a breath in agony and swallowed the cries of pain that wanted to tear out of my throat. If nothing else, I wouldn't give him the satisfaction. The cold rain felt like points of fire across my skin, and I shivered uncontrollably.

Even shirtless, it's hard to tell what gender I am. I am flat-chested with broad, heavy muscle across my torso. There's no question I was designed to fight. Even without exercise, I retain strength, and most of it is concentrated in my upper body to aid in the arts of war. Angels are built according to our purpose rather than aesthetics or sexual characteristics. Before I fell, I didn't have a gender. While I have come to understand I am female, biologically speaking, I walk the line between male and female in appearance. Few can tell which I am at first glance. Even my voice is neutral — too low to be identifiable as female, too high to be male.

If my companion cared about my physique, he showed no indication. Instead, he turned me so he could see my back easily and clicked his tongue against his teeth. "Brace yourself, angel. This will hurt."

He was right.

Raw pain flared across my back, following a narrow, focused line. I must have screamed, but I don't remember doing so. When it finished, he gave me a minute to breathe before it started all over again in another spot. He repeated the process several more times. After the last one, I was shaking so badly and was so dizzy I almost fell off the rock. However, the demon grabbed my shoulders and pulled me against him, holding me upright. It wasn't a comforting gesture, I didn't think. He offered no apology or consolation, merely held me while I tried to collect myself. That said, his hands were gentler than strictly necessary.

I don't know how long we sat there, but he seemed to sense the minute I was able to sit on my own because he pulled away and lifted a bag I hadn't noticed before. Putting it on the rock, he withdrew a large box of gauze and a roll of medical tape. "Can't have you staining a new shirt," he grumbled before more or less turning me into a mummy. He wasn't good at bandaging—not that it surprised me—but he was at least thorough. Once he'd finished, he fumbled me into a button-down shirt very similar to the one he was wearing, followed by a suit coat and a winter coat. All had wing slits.

"This seems excessive," I said, finding my voice again.

"If you're going to wear clothes at all, they should be decent ones. Honestly. Have you no sense of style?"

"I live under a bridge."

He wrinkled his nose. "Well, now you will live under a bridge in Armani."

"I don't think I know that place."

"Oh for the love of…"

The pain was starting to fade some as my body healed itself. While I don't heal as quickly as a were or some of the other similar species out there, I heal far faster than the average. Some of the lesser wounds were already closed, and now that my companion had stopped the worst of the bleeding, my head was clearer. Which brought me to a question I hadn't expected to ask: "What's your name?"

He raised a brow at me, then smirked. "Ah, so that you may banish me?"

I shook my head. "No."

Silence reigned for a long moment as he finished adjusting the buttons on my shirt and brushed imaginary dust off my coat. "You may call me Asakku." It wasn't his real, full name. It didn't have the ring of authenticity to it that celestial (or infernal) names carry. Of course, it would have been foolish for him to give up such a treasure so readily, but at least I had a means to address him now rather than just "demon," which felt rude. Why I cared about that, I couldn't tell you, but I did.

"Thank you, Asakku." The words tasted bitter on my lips. I knew this had to be a ruse. He was trying to manipulate me somehow. He had to be; it's what they do. Convince me to trust him so he could get what he wanted out of me. Then he would either kill me or vanish. Regardless of his motives, however, he *had* helped me, which deserved gratitude.

My thanks gave him as much pause as having to thank him gave me. We stared at each other for a long while before he nodded. "Yes, well. They were fools. You could've destroyed them yourself, I'm sure, but who am I to pass up an opportunity to get into the good graces of the city's very own avenging angel?" His cryptic smile returned with a brief, mocking bow that made me want to punch him.

"So why *were* you here conveniently just when I was attacked?" No small part of me suspected he'd set it up himself to create exactly this scenario.

"Because I'm stalking you, of course."

I hadn't expected him to be so blunt about it, and I did a double take. "You're *what?*"

"Come now. It's not every day a new fallen arrives on Earth."

"I have been here almost two years."

He chuckled in what I could almost mistake as genuine amusement. "Two years. As if that's longer than a hummingbird's wingbeat."

His laughter annoyed me, and I glared at him, trying to stand up. I got there, but the world tilted, and dizziness washed over me. Asakku guided me to sit back down, still chuckling. "Do stop taking yourself so seriously. That must be exhausting. Have you anybody you can call to come get you? As much as I find your consternation amusing, I do have other things to be doing beyond babysitting you."

"Then go," I snapped, probably less kindly than needed.

His smile vanished, and he lowered his hands. "If that is your wish. I will see you around, angel." Then, just as before, he was gone.

The minute he left, I felt guilty for what I'd said. I shouldn't have—he was a *demon*—but nonetheless, I did. I shook my head. No. He was trying to get me to feel that way. Trying to get me to let him in close. I wouldn't make that mistake again.

I fished my phone out of my jeans pocket and checked the time. It was only about 7:30 a.m., and I hated to wake Jim up, but Asakku had been right about me needing help. I pressed and held the button to speed-dial Jim and sighed as I held the phone to my ear.

Jim picked up on the second ring, his voice rough from sleep. "Cass. Everything okay?"

I didn't answer immediately, my throat tightening when I heard his voice.

"Cass, you there?" Jim sounded more alert now.

"Yes. Sorry. I'm not well."

"Where are you? I'll come get you." He was moving. I heard sounds in the background. Maybe he was dressing.

"It is not an emergency."

"You sound awful, emergency or not. Where are you?"

"Franklin Park."

"What *part* of Franklin Park?"

"Not sure. I ran a long way. I've never been here before." I squinted through the trees to my right where I heard the sound of traffic and could see a road. "Can I call you back?"

"Yeah. Get your bearings, then tell me where you are. I'm on my way."

"I am sorry for—"

"No." Jim cut me off, his voice stern. "No, Cassiel. This is what friends do. We take care of each other. Find out where you are, and I'll be there."

"Thank you."

"You're welcome. Now get me that road name."

We rang off, and I put the phone in my pocket. I was about to get up when I realized the cocktail umbrella was still in my coat pocket. The coat the demons had torn to ribbons. "No!" I didn't intend on saying anything, but the word tore itself out of me as I frantically looked around for the garment, but found nothing. The archdemon must have taken my destroyed clothing with him when he left. "No, no, no!" I patted myself down, grimacing as the wounds across my body pulled and burned.

In a last ditch effort, I shoved my hand into the coat pocket and felt a pill bottle.

I yanked the container out of my pocket and, to my infinite relief, saw the little umbrella inside. I hugged it to my chest as though it were more precious than gold—which to me, it was. Tears sprang to my eyes, and I tried to catch my breath. It was okay. I was damaged, but I would heal. Demon or not, I was all right. My shoulders shook as I cried, the adrenaline finally leaving me.

Not waiting for the tears to stop, I tried again to stand up. I made it to my feet, but I felt like I weighed about a hundred times more than I did. Swallowing hard, I wiped my face and made for the road.

It took me a minute to negotiate my way out of the enclosure and stagger through the trees. When I reached the road, an old stone wall dropped down onto a stone embankment. It was maybe fifteen feet down the incline to the sidewalk, but it looked like Mt. Everest with how tired I felt. A street sign told me I'd emerged onto Seaver Street.

I pulled out my phone and texted my location to Jim and sat on the stone wall, grateful for the coat the archdemon had given me. It fit me better than the other one had, I realized. So did the shirt. They didn't pull anywhere and felt like they'd been sewn for me in particular. That was impossible, of course, since he'd been gone all of three minutes. Though how he'd been able to figure out my exact size for clothing so quickly, I had no idea.

# CHAPTER 7

Jim arrived about fifteen minutes after I told him where I was, his van pulling up to the traffic light. By then, I felt strong enough to descend the embankment and managed to do so without falling. Barely. I reached the bottom, and Jim opened the passenger door for me. It took me a second to clamber in, which earned him some angry honking from nearby drivers upset that he took about eight seconds longer than they would have liked.

Jim ignored them until I was settled, then pulled away from the curb. While it was against the law for me not to wear a seatbelt, I couldn't tolerate the idea. The notion of anything touching my back made it ache, so I just slouched forward in the chair, leaning my hands on the dash.

Once we were under way, Jim looked over at me. "What happened, and why are you wearing such fancy clothes?"

I didn't have the energy to be delicate about it. I just blurted out the whole story while Jim listened and drove. My hands started to shake again as I talked about Asakku, though I didn't know why.

When I finished, I realized Jim had pulled over to the side of the road and parked in front of a playground while he listened. He reached over and took my hand in his, squeezing my fingers. "Breathe, Cass." His hand felt warm, solid, and strong against mine. "Breathe."

I did so, closing my eyes and taking a deep breath.

"Good. I'm going to take you back to my place so I can look you over. Okay? Then we'll figure out our next steps." His voice sounded so calm and sure. I nodded, grateful to let him make decisions for me in that moment. "I've got you, Cass. You don't have to go through this alone." His thumb moved over my knuckles slowly but with pressure.

"I'm sorry. I didn't want to drag you into—"

"No." There was that sharp tone again, and he pointed at me with his free hand. "We are friends, you stubborn ass. That means I have your back when things get hard. Just like you've got mine. Get that through your head. You, me, Eirlas, Dust—we're a squad, and we don't leave anyone behind. Stop apologizing for needing backup. It's what we're here for."

I withered a little and nodded, looking at the floor.

Jim squeezed my hand one more time then got us moving again, turning around to head back toward his apartment.

I didn't say anything during the drive, too wrapped up in my thoughts. When Jim pulled into his parking lot and turned the van off, I jumped as I looked around and realized where we were. "Sorry."

"What's with you, Cass? You're not usually so jumpy."

"I don't know. Just… something about all of this has me on edge." I opened the door and climbed out, waiting for Jim to disembark and roll around the back of his van.

When he did, we went into his apartment, where he pointed at one of his kitchen chairs. "Sit."

Jim's apartment was a studio located on the first floor of a brick building designed for disability access. The counters in the small kitchenette were lower than what I had come to understand was the standard, as was the sink in the bathroom. He also had a shower chair in the shower, something I'd used more than once when borrowing his shower. In addition to the kitchenette, the small living space housed his bed, a television, a small couch, and a recliner. The whole space was neat as a pin without a speck of dust to be seen anywhere. The secondhand furniture didn't match, but all of it was comfortable.

I sat where he indicated, and he rolled into his living room, reaching under his bed to pull out a backpack containing a well-stocked first aid kit. It and I were well acquainted. He returned and set the backpack on the table. "All right. Off with the jacket and shirt." It wasn't the first time he'd helped me like this, so the idea of removing my clothes around him didn't bother me. Honestly, nudity didn't bother me in general at that point in my life, and I didn't understand why people got so flustered about it.

He had to help me remove the clothes, and his brows rose when he glanced at the label inside the collar. "You mentioned he'd given you clothes. You didn't say they were Armani."

"What *is* Armani?" I asked, leaning my head on my hands.

"It's a clothing brand. This coat? Easily worth a grand. Maybe more. Really expensive clothing. Your shirt and jacket? Same sort of price."

"...Oh." I stared at him. "Can... can I store those here? I don't... I wouldn't have any way to..."

Jim held up his hands. "We'll deal with your clothes after I look at you." He got to removing the gauze. Jim was both more gentle and more skilled than Asakku had been, but even then, it hurt. As careful as he was, I was a mess, and we both knew it.

"You look like you got put through a food processor." Jim studied the cuts and gouges covering me.

"I sort of feel like that."

"I will never cease to be amazed at how much damage you can take and still be on your feet, Cassiel." He touched an uninjured place on my back. "Some of these look like they might get infected if we don't close them, though."

"I doubt it. I cannot get infections."

"Fair point. Either way, these need cleaning. Some of them have dirt wedged up in there." He sighed. "This... Asakku did probably save your life, much as I dislike the idea of giving a demon credit for anything. If I'm guessing right, you probably couldn't have closed some of these deeper ones fast enough to avoid bleeding out."

I hadn't told Jim how cold I'd felt or how close I'd come to blacking out. I'd just stuck to basic facts about the fight and what happened after. I didn't want to worry him, but I knew he was right. Instead of answering, I gave a noncommittal grunt. Which I knew Jim would understand and treat as an indication I didn't want to talk.

Jim got to cleaning and re-bandaging my back and shoulders before he helped me dress again. He loaned me a long-sleeved button-up and t-shirt rather than risking the ridiculously expensive clothing I'd been gifted. We both agreed it might be best to store it at Jim's since I had nowhere safe or clean to keep such things. Though why I was keeping it at all, I didn't know. The only part of it I decided to keep with me was the coat, which was both extremely warm and fit me well. Regardless of the clothing's origins, it was a pleasant upgrade. And I did need a new coat after what had happened to mine.

By the time we finished getting me put together again, it was almost 9 a.m., and Jim made breakfast. I wasn't hungry, but he insisted, so I didn't argue. I'd learned not to. Trying to argue with Jim was like fighting a force of nature. It just didn't work. He set a plate of scrambled eggs with two pieces of toast and a cup of very pale coffee in front of me before fixing an identical breakfast for himself. Though he took his coffee black.

"So, the gist of all this is, we're looking for a holy artifact that demons in the city want."

I nodded. "Before they get to it, yes."

"While I want to keep the boys in the loop, Eirlas and Dust won't be much help with this. But I do know someone who might be able to help you track this thing down."

"I'm all ears." I nudged eggs around my plate before forcing some down.

"I don't know him extremely well, but there's a PI I'm familiar with who's decent at finding lost things. He might at least know how to start tracking something like that down."

That surprised me. "He knows how to locate holy objects?"

Jim shook his head. "Not that specifically," he explained. "He's good at finding things no one else can, though. And if he doesn't know, he might know who we can talk to. It's at least a direction. I can't promise how much help he'll be."

"Something is better than nothing."

"That's what I thought."

We finished our breakfast, and Jim banished me to lie on the couch and rest. I heal quickly, but it never fails to exhaust me. Jim made a few phone calls while I watched television, trying to keep my mind off of all of this. And, most particularly, off of Asakku.

I flipped through channels until Jim rolled over to me. "We're meeting Axton at noon to discuss finding this thing, and you, me, Dust, and Eirlas are doing dinner together tonight. Also, Eirlas is going to get your things. You're staying here at least for tonight."

"What about Mrs. —"

Jim's expression darkened, his eyes going hard. "If she tries anything, she'll regret that choice." It wasn't a physical threat, of course, but I knew Jim could be as cutting with his words as he could with any weapon. Jim had been a Marine drill instructor, and I'd heard him bark at someone once. The memory stuck with me, however. He'd stopped a shooter high on demon-tainted drugs in their tracks by bellowing at them. "Until our meeting, you're staying on that couch and doing exactly nothing." He pointed at me.

I lifted my hands in surrender. This was one of the few times I had no desire to argue with his assessment.

# CHAPTER 8

St. Mary's lies at the eastern edge of Harambee Park, adjacent to a Civil War-era cemetery of the same name as the church. It is an old church. Old enough that it occupies real consecrated ground, which is one of my favorite parts of it. The church campus takes up almost a city block and is home to the church proper, an administration building—which also houses the meeting rooms—the Sunday school, a shelter and soup kitchen, the rectory, and a small playground for the children. I lived there in a converted janitor's closet for over a year before the previous priest, Father John Carver, died at the hands of a demon. It was as close to a home as anything I'd found since my fall.

We arrived at the church a few minutes before our scheduled meeting, and Jim and I headed to Jim's office. His office occupied a slice of the first floor of the administration building, which had easy wheelchair access. While it was small, it was comfortable enough. The space held Jim's desk, two chairs across from it, and a metal cabinet along with some wall-mounted bookshelves. A window behind the desk looked out into the church's courtyard and playground.

Jim rolled behind his desk, and I sat down in one of the two chairs, fidgeting. He must have noticed because Jim gave me a smile as he booted up his computer. "It's all right, Cass. Axton is... Well, he's a good enough man. Just be cautious what you say about angels and demons and such around him."

"So he's not a believer."

"To be honest, I'm not sure."

"Then why are we hiring *him* to help us find a holy relic?"

"Because he's good at finding things. Whether he believes it is what it is or not, he'll do the work."

"And you intend on paying him for this?"

Jim nodded. "I might not be able to pay for everything we might want, but he should be able to help us get started, anyway."

"So it is expensive."

"Let's just focus on our goal, shall we?"

I sighed. Jim and the others had spent more money on me than I cared to think about over the time I'd known them, and it had never sat well with me. However, I knew I couldn't get a job without identification, and I couldn't get that without a lot of paperwork I just didn't have. After all, "fell from the sky" isn't exactly a legal immigration method.

About ten minutes later, a broad, tall man filled the doorway. He had olive-dark skin, black hair, and slate-gray eyes and carried enough muscle that most people would think twice about starting a fight with him. A short, scruffy beard covered his jaw as though he'd started trying to shape it once but gave up soon after. He wore a black duster over blue jeans and a gray Henley that fit close to his chest, highlighting his bulk.

"Hammerson," he said, his voice low and gravelly. He gave Jim a nod of greeting, and Jim returned it. The exchange had the curt, efficient manner I had come to expect of military folk.

"Graves. Come in. Close the door, would you?" He waved a hand at the free chair across from him.

Axton nodded and stepped into the office, closing the door and dropping into the seat beside mine. He gave me a once-over, but it felt more perfunctory than anything, and his focus settled on Jim again. "So, what's the situation?"

Jim gestured to me with a jerk of his chin. "This is Cassiel. Cass for short. I'm hiring you on her behalf."

This time, Axton's study was more focused as he turned in his chair to examine me more closely. "All right."

I met his gaze for a moment before answering. There was a weight to the way he looked at me, the gray eyes piercing and intent now. I became intensely aware of how beat-up I looked and felt after my earlier fight with the demons. "Are you a believer?" I asked, not sure how to start the explanation.

"If you start trying to recruit me, I'm going to leave." He shifted his weight as though to stand. "C'mon, Jim, you know that's not my scene."

"No. No, please stay. It is… revelent."

"Relevant." Jim corrected me with a slight smile.

"Relevant," I repeated, closing my eyes and taking a slow, deep breath, annoyed with myself.

Axton's jaw tensed, and he squinted at me, his expression hard. It felt personal. "My relationship with the Big Guy has been rocky for a long time. I like the Catholic church even less."

"But you believe."

He grunted in a way I took as an assent.

"I have reason to believe there is an artifact in the city. Something the forces of evil want. I need to find it before they do."

"Artifact. Judging by your pussy footing around the subject, I assume you mean a holy relic. Something of religious power?"

"Holy power. Yes." It was hard not to look away from the gaze he'd trapped me in, but I felt that retreating from it would signal weakness I couldn't afford to display in that moment.

"What's it to you?" he asked, not batting an eye at the idea of a holy relic. Still, that stare pierced me, as though he could see through my skin and down into my soul.

"I want to prevent them from getting it."

"You know this sounds like the plot of a movie, right?" Axton said, crossing his arms and leaning back in his chair. "Tell me it's not the *Da Vinci Code* or something."

I had no idea what that was and looked to Jim for help.

"You don't have to believe it in order to help us find something," Jim said. "But this is important to us, and we're paying."

Axton sighed and shook his head, closing his eyes and taking a slow breath before releasing it just like I had a moment before. "All right. What are you looking for, and where was it last seen?"

"I don't know the answer to the second question," I said. "But the first one, it's one of the nails from the cross. I have learned it is here in Boston and that there are…" I trailed off, not sure what to say. "Bad people after it," I finished, knowing the explanation was woefully short of the true gravity of the situation.

"Because of course there are," Axton said with a roll of his eyes. "All right. So you have no idea where this artifact is or when it arrived in the city? If it's in the city at all?"

I shook my head. "No. Which I know makes this difficult."

"First thing we do is see if there's a register somewhere with who has what where. Usually, things like that are announced to the public since they want people to come see them. Pieces of the saints and so on." He rubbed his forehead and pulled out his phone. "I'll see what I can dig up. I'm going to need you to come by my office and fill out some paperwork before I start, though. I didn't bring it with me since I wasn't sure what we were looking at."

"Then why didn't we just meet at your office?" Jim asked, raising a brow.

Axton shrugged. "I was going to be in the area anyway on another job. Figured we could talk a little in person before formalizing anything. We've known each other a while, Hammerson. You're a good guy, so I try to make time. Besides, the parking around my office isn't easy to navigate your van into, so I figured I'd save you a trip if I couldn't help."

"Ah, well, thanks," Jim said. "Would it work if you gave me a quote over the phone, and I sent Cass with a check?"

"Yeah." Axton nodded. "That'll work. Come by my office tomorrow. Noon. That work for you?" He handed me a business card he pulled out of his wallet.

"Yes." I had no idea where his office was, but I could figure it out, and Jim could give me directions, I was sure.

"All right." He stood up, offering Jim a hand. "Nice to see you again, Hammerson." Jim shook his hand. When they finished, Axton turned toward me.

I stood, discovering he and I were similar in height, with Axton perhaps less than an inch taller. He had a bit more bulk than I did as well, but again, not by much.

He held his hand out to me, and I shook it. His grip was strong and unyielding, but he made no effort to crush my fingers. I matched it—something I had learned from Dust—and instinctively squared my shoulders. Axton wasn't attempting to intimidate or overpower me, but I could tell every action was an assessment of some kind. Why I was different than Jim, I didn't know, but I could feel him trying to get a read on me. "Cass, was it?" he said.

"Yes."

"I'll see you tomorrow." Axton released the handshake and headed to the door.

After he'd left, I sat back down, frowning as I replayed the conversation in my head. "Did I do something wrong?" I asked, looking at Jim.

Jim shrugged. "He's not usually so," he paused, "intense. I don't know what that was about." The expression on Jim's face mirrored mine as he looked at the door. "At least not when he isn't in the middle of a tough job. I've only met him a few times, but that was a little weird."

"Maybe he doesn't like me."

"I can't see why." Jim gave me a smile. "You're very likable."

I smiled a little. "Thanks, Jim." His kind words didn't do anything to chase away my concern, however. A small knot of anxiety formed in my gut at the idea of meeting Axton alone the next day.

# CHAPTER 9

We spent the rest of the afternoon at the church. I didn't have the energy to do much of anything but sit in his office while Jim did whatever he did on his computer. I knew nothing about computers at the time and had never really used one. Father John had tried to show me a few things before he died, but we determined I was more or less hopeless with them. So Jim's sitting in front of one for hours was like magic to me. I had no idea what he could possibly be doing, but I respected him too much to bother him with questions.

Instead, I read one of the books I'd pulled off his shelf. Jim had told me his favorite was *The Lion, The Witch, and the Wardrobe*, and since I was to sit there while he worked and had nothing to do with myself, he'd pointed toward his bookshelves and suggested I read. Reading, he'd told me, would help both with my vocabulary and with my understanding of the world overall.

Around five in the afternoon, Jim stretched and glanced at his watch. "We're due to meet Eirlas and Dust for dinner soon. You ready to go?"

I lifted my head, drawn out of the other world by his voice. "Oh. Yes." It took me a few minutes to put my head together. Reading fiction wasn't something I had done before, and drawing myself back into the real world felt like when I'd accidentally turned the water on too cold in Jim's shower.

I closed the book, hungry to know how the story ended, and stood, putting it back on Jim's shelf.

"You can borrow it if you like," he offered, giving me a knowing smile.

"If something happened to it, I could not replace it."

A laugh escaped him, and Jim shook his head. "I can always buy another copy. It's not expensive."

"If you are…" I grunted. "If *you're* certain."

"I am." He rolled around his desk. "How are you feeling?"

"Still very stiff, but better. I think some of the deeper wounds may take me a few days to heal, but the lesser ones are fading." I rolled my shoulders, hissing in a breath between my teeth as I assessed my condition. "I shouldn't fight more demons tonight, but I can manage dinner."

"If you're sure. We can always do takeout at my place."

"I am all right."

Jim studied me, though it wasn't in the same, cold manner Axton had, and nodded. He led me out of the church to his van, and we mounted up. "They're meeting us at the restaurant."

"Where are we going?"

"An orcish restaurant. One of Dust's favorites. It's not too far from here." Jim put the car into gear and hit the road, driving a short way north around the edge of Franklin Park and then onto one of the branching side streets nearby.

Ogtso was a small restaurant huddled just off the main thoroughfare. It resembled a diner, and likely the building had been one once. Plastic and metal chairs and tables mostly designed for larger denizens were jammed up against each other with a long steam table against the back wall. While it didn't look like much, if Dust vouched for it, the food was probably incredible.

Despite living in project housing with Eirlas, Dust worked in the kitchen of one of the higher-end restaurants of Boston. He never said which, and I never asked. Why he wouldn't say, I couldn't tell you. His taste in food, however, is impeccable. I would have thought working in a fancy place would have come with a good paycheck, but Dust never seemed to have much money. I didn't ask what he did with what he had, but I knew he and Eirlas didn't have a great deal between them.

Dust and Eirlas were already seated when we entered the place, the two of them having claimed a table designed for humans rather than orcs. While Dust looked squeezed into the space, I knew he had chosen it because Jim couldn't have reached the higher tables comfortably. Nor could Eirlas or I.

The pair waved at us, brilliant smiles lighting their faces.

Aside from Jim, Dust and Eirlas were the two closest friends I had. Dust was a large orc with mottled green skin and black hair he kept shaved close to his head in the same military style as Jim. His eyes were dark and usually warm, despite his gruff nature and tendency to bark at people. He had served in the military some time ago but wouldn't say more than that about it. Like most of the former military I'd met thus far.

Conversely, Eirlas was a slender, almost delicate-looking elf covered in tattoos. I had learned they were some sort of gang symbols, but I still didn't know what they meant. He had white-blonde hair which he wore long and kept tied back from his face.

The two had started dating a few months ago, and their happiness buoyed me in difficult times. Generally, elves and the tusked races (orcs, ogres, and trolls) didn't get along. Eirlas hadn't given me an in-depth explanation, but it involved World War II and an attempt at ethnic cleansing. The races still didn't get along well, despite the intervening time. And yet here they were, madly in love.

"You made it!" Dust said as we approached the table. "Good to see you."

While he still ran the soup kitchen at the church, my living arrangements meant I didn't see Dust as often as I once had. I still caught him a couple times a week, but service was so busy we didn't have much of a chance to talk. That said, he checked in as often as he could. I saw Eirlas even less since he worked with the shelter, and I no longer stayed there.

Eirlas smiled at us as well. "Hey." Elves, as a race, are supernaturally beautiful, and he was no different. His smile could almost literally light up a room, and his angular features made most people who saw him blush. Even with the tough-looking tattoos, he remained stunning, and the honesty of his manner could make anybody feel safer around him. He and Dust were near-complete opposites, but something about the two of them just *fit*.

Jim and I joined them with Jim taking the empty space where Dust must have had them remove a chair for him. "How are you both?" I asked, looking between them.

"Good. Been busy, but we're keeping things going. Been running into some trouble at the church, though," Dust answered, shaking his head.

"Trouble?" Jim raised a brow.

"Someone told Father Demoyne about us." Eirlas said it quietly, his gaze lowering to the table. "He's been saying that if we continue to 'live in sin,' he's going to relieve us of our duties."

"So get married?" I asked, not understanding the issue.

Jim patted my shoulder. "It's not that, Cass." A slow, deep sigh left him. "It's because they're gay."

I scoffed. "The Father doesn't care about that. Why should that fool of a priest?"

"He claims the Bible says—" Dust started.

I cut him off. "You know exactly what I think of Father Demoyne's interpretation of the Bible." On more than one occasion, I had nearly come to blows with the priest over the subject. It had gotten so bad, the three of them had decided to never leave me alone with Father Demoyne. Which, thinking about it, was one of their better decisions.

"Be that as it may," Jim said, his hand still on my shoulder, "he can still cause trouble for us."

"I think perhaps we pray for a new priest or look for a church," Eirlas said with a deep sigh, looking at the rest of us.

Dust shook his head. "I'm staying and fighting. Before Demoyne, that church was home. The people there need us. We can't just walk away."

"Then we fight." I nodded.

Food arrived, and I blinked in surprise. Usually, ordering had to happen before food came. Even I knew that.

My confusion must have shown on my face because Dust laughed. "I ordered for you since I doubted you'd know what to order," he explained, gesturing to the dishes.

Orcish cooking is reminiscent of English fare since they largely come from the British Isles. A lot of savory pies, roasts, sausages, and hearty foods mostly seasoned with herbs and spices common to the spaces they inhabited.

The two things you need to know about orcish cooking are: everything not sweet probably has garlic, nettle, and elder in it in generous portions, and most sweet things have mint or berries; and their food comes in orcish portions. Which means you're taking some home unless you can eat like one (or, you know, are one).

There wasn't much conversation over dinner as we all mulled over what to do about the church. After a while, Jim spoke up. "There's also another problem."

I sighed. This was the part of the conversation I had least wanted to broach. Dust and Eirlas knew what I was, and they had stood with me against a demon in the past. Nonetheless, I wanted to avoid bringing them into this mess if I could. Particularly since I didn't know exactly what, who, or where threats were coming from. Last time, we had gotten lucky. While the demon had been an archdemon, it hadn't been one of significant power for an arch — likely having come from one of the less potent choirs of angels — and we had managed to surprise it.

Jim explained what little we knew about the artifact, its origins, and our intent to hire Axton to try and locate it. Dust went pale and stared at the table as Jim laid it all out, hunching forward in his seat and resting his folded arms on the table. When Eirlas touched his elbow, he jumped so hard, his seat groaned beneath him.

I didn't blame him.

The last time we'd dealt with demons, Dust had been possessed, and those kinds of scars didn't fade quickly. He'd been aware of the demon's movements and plans while it occupied him, which was how we'd located our enemy. That awareness came with a price since being a spectator in your own body while a demon forces you to do things you otherwise wouldn't was undoubtedly traumatizing.

"I'm not asking for you two to do anything," I said, breaking in. "Right now, we do not know enough to act anyway. And with any luck, you will not need to be involved."

Jim caught my eye and nodded. "She's right. I just felt you should know what's afoot."

"Our situation is not a foot. It's not any body part."

The three laughed. "Afoot means happening or what's going on, Cass," Eirlas said.

I grumbled and tried to hide my embarrassment in the remains of my pie. Which only prompted more laughter.

At least it had broken the tension.

After the moment of levity, Dust leaned a burly arm on the table. "So, what does this thing do? I get that it's important. Wouldn't want demons getting hold of a napkin, let alone a nail of the cross, but you're acting like this is some kind of WMD or something."

"Weapon of mass destruction," Eirlas cut in when he caught the beginnings of my perplexed expression.

I chewed on the inside of my lip, trying to figure out how much to tell them. Mortals are only meant to know so much. "From ancient times, and even some modern, there are… items in the world that carry potent holy power. Things touched by angels, and even God Himself. Or the Son. These items are capable of incredible feats. I am sure you know of the parting of the Red Sea. Moses' staff was one such object. Something with the capacity to part the waters on that magnitude and drown an army was of significance. The nails can be used in similar ways. I do not know exactly what powers they hold since relics weren't my purview, but… if there really is one here, and if we are really facing demons trying to abscond with them, I fear what they may intend to do. These nails have come into direct contact with the blood of the divine. You cannot imagine the power they hold.

"For all I know, the enemy might try to corrupt it somehow and use it in a rite to, perhaps, try and tear a hole into Heaven and start another war."

"Another war?" Jim asked

I gave him a sidelong look. "The initial fall of Lucifer and his supporters is hardly the only battle between angels and demons that has happened. We just do not tend to talk about the others. That said, the few major fights that *have* occurred on or in proximity to Earth have caused tremendous damage to the world. Not every major disaster can be blamed on us, but things like the Black Plague, ice ages, and other such natural cataclysms are sometimes indicators of such things. Or large wars. It's not always caused by a celestial conflict happening — we are not responsible for the actions of mortal creatures directly — but sometimes, the war pours over the edge and affects other things. Demons in particular like to involve mortals because they know how much it upsets and angers the angelic host."

"So what you're saying is there's a nuke loose in Boston, and the bad guys are after it," Dust said with a nod.

"I think this is a little bigger than a microwave."

All three of them stared at me in blank confusion for a very long time before Eirlas tried to explain. One of these days, I will understand why words in the mortal language do not mean just one thing. Today was not that day.

# CHAPTER 10

By the way, Cass," Dust said after everyone finished having their chuckle at my expense, "I have someone I want you to meet. An old buddy of mine from the service. He runs a shop and mentioned he was looking for help."

"I can't work," I said, lifting my hands. "I don't have an ID or, well, anything else."

"Not gonna be a problem here. T's a good guy. He'll take care of you."

"His name is tea?"

"T's short for Tremor."

"That's a strange name."

"Tremor?"

I nodded.

Dust smirked and looked at Jim. "Pretty common to get nicknames in the military. Jim was 'The Hammer' when he was a DI. And it's why I go by 'Dust.'"

"That isn't your real name?" I asked, feeling as though I'd missed something. "What is your real name, then?"

He shook his head. "I don't go by it, so it doesn't matter. Tomorrow, after your meeting with Graves, I've told him you're coming by his shop."

"I suppose. Where does he work?"

"About two or three miles from where you've been staying. Easy flight."

"That should not be bad." I nodded, not wanting to think about the injuries I'd sustained and that it might, in fact, be more trouble than I cared to admit.

"Shouldn't," Eirlas pointed out.

"Shouldn't," I echoed with a sigh.

"Can you fly with how torn up you are?" Jim asked, frowning in my direction. Trust him to always say the quiet part out loud when it came to things like this.

"I should be able to, but I'll make that decision after I've rested." I said the last part to placate him, knowing Jim would badger me if I didn't.

He raised a brow in my direction as if he could smell the defiance on me. "Good." Jim pointed at me with his fork, giving me a narrow-eyed look. "And make sure it's a *smart* decision, Cass."

I opened my mouth to protest, but Jim just stared, daring me to fight with him on it. I shut it again, and he went back to eating.

"That reminds me," Eirlas said, reaching under the table between his feet. "I got your bag." He produced the beaten-up backpack I used and offered it to me.

"Thank you." I accepted it and set the backpack down at my side. A thought occurred to me, and I tilted my head some, studying Eirlas's arms and hands. "How much does it cost to get a tattoo?"

Eirlas did a bit of a double take. "Uh, depends. What do you want a tattoo for?"

I pulled the pill bottle with my beloved umbrella out of my pocket. "I am afraid to lose this. It is important to me. If I get a tattoo of it, I cannot lose it."

The four of us looked at the little bottle for a moment in silence. Father John had been something different for each of us, but he had been important to all of us. That, and his death had opened the door for Father Demoyne, who could not have been more different than Father John if he'd tried.

Eirlas broke the silence. "Depends on how big you want it and where. Do you know?"

I shook my head. "I don't really know, but it doesn't need to be big. I want it somewhere I can see it, though."

He chewed his lip in consideration, looking more through me than at me, before he nodded. "Maybe your forearm or wrist, then. You could see it whenever you wanted, but it wouldn't be too big. It also wouldn't be too expensive. I'll ask around some of the studios I know and see what they'd charge."

"Thank you. Perhaps if I begin working for this 'Tremor' person, I will have money to buy one."

Jim stretched some and popped his back. "I should get Cass home. For all she might not agree with it, she needs to get some sleep. That meeting tomorrow won't have itself."

Whatever that meant.

We parted ways after cautious and gentle hugs, and Eirlas promised again to get me some quotes. Dust gave me Tremor's phone number and said to give him a call after I finished meeting with Axton. Jim took me back to the apartment and encouraged me to rest. He'd been right. I was exhausted.

---

The next day, I slept very late. Jim didn't wake me until it was nearly time for my meeting with Graves, and when he did, it was with a plate of eggs, bacon, sausages, beans, and fried tomatoes. He didn't say anything, but I knew he had put it together because we'd been talking about Father John. If there was one thing most of the parish had known about him, it was his fondness for a good "Full English."

Jim wasn't much of a cook, but the food was good, and we sat together at his little kitchen table in silent communion over the memory of our departed friend.

My back still hurt, but the worst of the pain had deadened. When we finished eating, Jim had me strip my shirt off to take a look at how things were healing.

"Most of these are looking pretty good." His fingertips moved over my shoulders, tracing the lines of fading wounds. "This one's still pretty nasty, though." He paused at one of the gouges that had bled the most. "I'll bandage it back up for you. I don't know how you aren't reacting more to these, Cass. Do you just not feel pain like everyone else?"

"I do not know how much things hurt for you, but they very much hurt me."

"Just soldiering through, huh?" he asked while he worked, cutting gauze to the proper size and creating a cushion of it between me and the tape. And my clothes.

I yawned. "If that means to continue on as a soldier would, yes."

"That's exactly what it means." He nodded. "Remember, you're meeting with Dust's friend after your meeting with Axton."

"I don't think Axton likes me very much. Are you sure he'll help?" I asked, stumbling a little over the contractions but managing to remember to use them. It was getting easier with time, but I still had to think about it when I was tired or in pain. And at that moment, I was both.

"Whether he likes you or not, he knows his business, and I'm paying him. That said, Graves is a good guy. I don't know if he likes you or not for whatever reason, but he's good people. Doesn't always act like it, but he is."

"Not everyone good acts it all the time," I said, thinking of Dust, who could get rather demanding and very grouchy in the kitchen while he worked. I knew it was just his manner and had learned to accept it from him.

"Nope. They don't. Which is why we have to look past the surface sometimes. Same thing with nice people. Someone nice can be rotten to the core while someone unfriendly might have a heart of gold."

"If someone had a heart made of gold, they would die," I said, frowning.

Jim sighed and rubbed a hand over his face. "It's a saying, Cass," he explained with a groan. "It means they're a good, generous, kind person. Gold is a precious metal. It means their heart is a valuable, rare, and precious thing. Not literal gold."

"Oh." All these turns of phrase annoyed me. Particularly since they often made no sense whatsoever. This one, I could piece together. A heart made of a precious metal. Something of worth. But some other phrases just confused me. I had learned not to think too deeply on them because if I did, it made my head hurt.

Jim finished his work, and I dressed. "Thank you."

"You're welcome. You going to be okay meeting him solo?"

"Yes, I think so." I rolled my shoulders and stretched, testing the bandaging. It pulled some, but it wasn't terrible. "I should be well enough to return to sleep in my usual space tonight. Thank you."

"Yeah. I'm sorry. I wish..." Jim trailed off and shook his head with a deep sigh before he went to throw away the used bandages and put his med kit to rights.

I put my hand on his back as he worked. "It's not your fault, you know." His guilt over not being able to let me stay was palpable. I knew it plagued him. "I have what I need." I squeezed his shoulder.

"I know that. But it still... it's so... ugh!" Jim jammed things into his med kit and shoved it under the bed with more force than necessary, his motions frustrated and jerky. I didn't blame him for it. I understood well the fury of facing a world that so often seemed as though it didn't truly care for its own.

"Whatever happens, Jim, I know you have done your best to help me and others. The Father has a place at his side for you, just as he did Father John. I know you often feel as though you are not doing enough. Faith without works is dead, but Jim... you work so hard." I ignored the pain and leaned over him, wrapping my arms around his shoulders. "It is enough," I said in his ear.

All the tension bled from him, and Jim sagged in my arms, leaning into the embrace. One of his hands lifted and rested to mine, and he squeezed it tightly, his fingers trembling ever so slightly.

# CHAPTER 11

A
xton's office was easy enough to find. Jim had given me directions and printed me a map from one of the church's computers that showed a direct route alongside the check he put in an envelope. He refused to let me see the numbers on it. The office was toward the center of town, down an alley off a side street buried between two buildings. Were I to guess, it helped to keep his rent low since he had no main street advertising, and finding him from the ground would've been a challenge. I landed with a grunt of discomfort on the cracked pavement in a cramped parking lot outside the address I'd been given and double-checked it, unsure I was in the right place. My back ached, as did... well, all of me. I regretted the flight, but I wasn't wrong about it being the fastest and most effective means of transport.

His office faced the alley at a ninety-degree angle from another business whose door sported the name "Memoriam Inc." in peeling white stickers on the inside of the window on the door. The buildings around me soared upward, blocking most of the sunlight and leaving the sky a small square of blue above me. I drew a breath and walked around the corner, finding Axton's door labeled in similar stickers that read, "Igneous Investigations."

A tiny waiting room with several chairs that had definitely been either secondhand or been in the office since the 1970s lay beyond the door. They looked comfortable but didn't match at all. A coffee table near them held out-of-date periodicals of various flavors and types. The only real nicety was a fountain occupying a corner of the room. It was about four feet tall and had been made of some kind of dark, heavy stone.

The door into Axton's office had a cracked frosted glass door, beyond which I could make out movement. Beside the door, mounted to the wall, was a small button resembling a doorbell. A note in square, blocky lettering said to "ring for service."

I checked the time on my cell phone and nodded. I was on time, so I walked up and pushed the button before retreating from the door.

Nothing happened for several minutes. Maybe I'd been wrong about the movement inside? I checked the time again and the piece of paper Jim had given me with the location and date on it, just to make sure. It all matched up to here and now.

A short time later, the door to the office opened, and a woman marched through the waiting room. Her eyes were red and puffy, and she sniffled a few times as she left. I stood, wondering if I should say something or try and help, but Axton's broad frame filled the doorway. "Sorry about that," he said with a sigh. "Had to deliver some bad news."

He looked tired, and his hair needed combing. The clothes he wore looked like he'd slept in them, too. Maybe he had. I frowned. "I am... sorry to hear that."

"Not as sorry as she is." He gestured toward the door in a vague manner without explaining further. "Come in. Let's talk about this job of yours." Axton stepped back from the door and walked into his office.

I followed.

Much the same as the waiting room, Axton's office was an eclectic mix of furniture. Two mismatched chairs sat in front of a beaten-up metal desk. The desk held a laptop, a coffee mug the size of my head, a notebook with some pens, and a forward-facing business card holder with cards matching the one in my pocket. Off to the side of the room, near the door, stood a small table which held a coffee maker that used those little single-use cups. Alongside were paper cups as well as a couple holding cream and sugar cups.

Against the far wall, away from the desk, an old couch with a coffee table in front of it sagged a little in a comfortable way. A heavy blanket lay folded neatly across the back, and several pillows suggested he slept there at least part of the time. Behind his desk hung several framed documents I couldn't make heads or tails of (but they looked important) as well as a number of newspaper clippings with headlines about missing persons found or important items retrieved. Some were yellowed with age, but others looked more recent.

"Sit." Axton gestured to the two chairs in front of his desk as he settled behind it, nudging the laptop out of the way in favor of the notebook and a pen.

I sat, not sure what he wanted to know.

"I know you and Jim told me most of it yesterday, but let's go over this again." He clicked the top of the pen and opened to a fresh page. "You go by Cassiel, that right?"

"Yes."

He wrote it down. "All right, so…"

I wrestled with how much to tell him. What to tell him. Jim wouldn't have sent me to someone who couldn't help, but I knew there was a significant chance he wouldn't believe me and might even refuse if I told him too much. I looked down at my hands and picked at the skin around my thumb where it was rough.

Axton waited, still as a statue and just as silent. It gave me the impression he did that a lot. Waiting, I mean.

A sigh left me, and I rubbed my hands over my face. "I know I asked yesterday, but are you a believer?"

"The Big Guy and I don't see eye-to-eye."

"That's not what I asked."

Axton grunted. "I'm not a churchgoer, but I've seen enough to know there are things bigger'n me in the world."

Would that be enough? I didn't know. "We are looking for something much bigger than both of us," I said, choosing my words carefully. "There is a relic in the city. An item of incredible power. There are…" I trailed off, not sure how to explain it. "The forces of evil are attempting to claim it. I intend to stop them."

The pen clicked, and Axton sat back in his chair, the movement drawing my gaze back to him. Again, he stared at me with hard eyes, like he could see down into my soul. "Yeah. You said as much yesterday. I want to make something very clear here, Cassiel: I don't work for the church. So if you're representing—"

I shook my head. "I'm not. I… I don't know that I represent anything or anyone. I did once. But now, I am just me."

He grunted. "So what's your interest in this so-called relic, then? What is it? Where is it?"

"I don't know where it is. Only that it is here." The rough skin around my thumb started bleeding, and I frowned at it. "As to what it is, it is a nail from the cross."

Axton took a slow, deep breath and closed his eyes for a few seconds. "You didn't say what you wanted with it."

"To keep it from falling into the wrong hands."

"Nothing else?"

I shook my head. "No. I have no designs on such a thing and would not even know what to do with it. I just don't want it to fall into the hands of those who would use it to harm people."

He studied me again. "All right, well, there are a lot of nails in Boston. I'm not sure how much help I can be. Not because I'm unwilling to take the job, but because I can't walk around the city making guesses. Also, who are these 'forces of evil'?"

I picked at my thumb again, frowning and trying to figure out how to explain it.

When I didn't answer, Axton pulled out a pack of black, sweet-smelling cigarettes from his pocket and lit one. It didn't smell like other cigarette smoke, and I had no idea what it was. Later, I learned they were called cloves. "Let's cut the bullshit," he said around the cigarette. "You think there are demons after it."

The words hit me like a bucket of cold water, and I looked at him. "You—"

He held up a hand. "Cassiel? The name's a dead giveaway. Plus, you don't have a last name. Whatever metaphor you've got here, how do I know any of this is legit? Jim's a friend, which is why I'm willing to hear you out, but are you, y'know, stable?"

The anxiety I'd felt melted into anger. "I am not insane!" I snapped, glaring at him. Usually when I did that, people quailed and retreated. The only person I'd yelled at who didn't flinch was Jim. And that was, I suspected, because he knew I wouldn't hurt him.

Axton didn't react, his gray eyes boring into mine. "When Father John died, you were the primary suspect in his murder. You weren't charged because they never found evidence, but you have to know how it looks. You told them demons did it. Demons. In a church. Detective Greene was pretty sure you weren't all there. He didn't think you'd killed anyone. Still doesn't, last I talked to him. But he's the only one."

When he mentioned the name, my mind conjured up the memory of the solemn-faced Black officer I'd interacted with at the station. While he had questioned me hard, he hadn't been unkind, nor had he laughed at me when I'd talked about demons. It had been a while ago, but I still recalled him. "What is their suspicion supposed to mean to me?" I asked, defaulting into the more formal speech I was most comfortable in.

"Mean?" Axton asked, raising a brow. "It doesn't have to mean anything to you. But it does mean something to me. The only reason we're even talking is because Jim vouched for you. You're telling me you didn't kill Father John?" he asked, his expression unreadable. Stone.

"No. He was my closest friend. I would not kill him. I could not have killed him. I was not even in the room when it happened. If I had been, I could have done something. Maybe I could have saved him." I shot to my feet, still glaring, my voice growing louder. "I came here because I was told you could help me. Not to be treated like… like this!"

"Sit down," Axton said, taking another draw of his cigarette.

"No. I will not be treated this way. I am an angel of the Lord, not some petty murderer." I snarled the words before I could censor them.

# CHAPTER 12

A xton and I stared at each other in silence for a long time, me trying to get my emotions under control, him just watching, expression unreadable.

"If you *are* an angel, what are you doing in my office?" he asked, finishing the first cigarette and starting a second. He put the first one out in the palm of his hand and tossed the butt of it into a garbage can.

"Exactly what I told you I was here for." I threw my hands up, frustration building in my chest. I wished Jim were here. He could have helped me communicate better than I did on my own. There was a good reason I avoided talking to people much. I never seemed to be able to make myself understood. I was too blunt. Too straightforward. I didn't pussyfoot around things enough. Worse, when others were unclear or sidestepped things, I became lost.

"No." He shook his head, still sitting in his chair, apparently unbothered by my outburst. "That's not what I meant. If you are a real angel, why are you in my office rather than…" he trailed off and gestured upwards.

I grit my teeth. "I am fallen."

"I see." He didn't react to the information any more than he had anything else. I had the feeling I could have told him I was a chimera and it would have had the same impact. He sighed and closed his eyes for a moment again, the only sign of emotion I'd seen from him so far. "Aren't fallen angels usually working for the side of Hell?"

My fingers curled into fists, and I stuffed them into my coat pockets. "I am not." It wasn't an unfair question, but knowing that didn't help the seething rage building in the pit of my stomach.

"Prove it."

I blinked, frowning at him. "You do not wish me to prove it."

"I do, actually," Axton said. "Father Demoyne thinks you're unhinged. And probably a heretic." It seemed he'd taken the intervening time since we'd met to do a thorough dig into my time in the world, and for some reason, that annoyed me. I should have expected it with his being an investigator, but the idea that he'd be studying *me* caught me off guard.

It had been a long few days. I was tired, my back still ached, I was worried about this artifact and the demons involved, and now this mortal creature was pushing my buttons so hard, he was fit to break them. It took all of my self control not to leap across the desk and punch him. It would, I reminded myself, not help me prove I was neither insane nor working on the side of Hell. "Father Demoyne is an idiot," I hissed through clenched teeth.

Axton's brows twitched, and he nodded in assent. "Be that as it may."

"You are sure you wish to see proof?"

"Oh yeah." He nodded again. "Lay it on me." Axton leaned forward, his cocky expression containing an eagerness I didn't entirely understand and was eager to wipe away.

My mouth curled up in one corner in a sarcastic little smile. "Be not afraid."

Holy fire curled up my body under my clothing, and my wings opened through the wing slits in my shirt and jacket, the six of them appearing from my neck, shoulders, and lower back. His office, which had been dimly lit by a failing fluorescent light overhead, was thrown into stark relief as white and blue light poured off my body.

The first time I'd revealed myself to Jim, he'd averted his eyes. Eirlas and Dust had nearly fallen out of their chairs. They were the only ones I'd shown myself to, but their reactions were, as far as I understood it, the usual fare. There is, after all, a reason angels always tell mortal creatures to "be not afraid" when we reveal ourselves. We are, by all accounts, terrifying beings.

Axton, on the other hand, squinted against the bright light and crossed his arms. His eyes, usually a dark gray, flickered with blue light, reflecting my Grace. I could feel him absorbing the power, resonating with it like a tuning fork. Nothing I had encountered so far had reacted that way, and the sensation gave me pause. I studied him with more respect than I had a moment ago. Whatever he was, Axton Graves was not human.

He drew a deep breath as if he'd not done so in ages, and a tremor went through him. A moment of stillness and silence came over him before he relaxed again. "All right," he said. "You can ditch the light show, seraph." Axton sighed, smoke coiling from his lips like a dragon's breath. "I believe you."

Ah. So he did know. I put my wings away, having been careful not to knock anything over with them, and doused the flames covering me. "Usually, I get more of a reaction."

"Usually, you are dealing with people who haven't seen a whole lot of angels." He chained a third cigarette. "So. The question is now: what *dumbfuck* decided to stick a holy relic with that kind of juice in Boston of all places? Most of those things are locked up in vaults in places like the Vatican."

The change in his attitude was so quick my head spun. "You aren't…" I trailed off.

"I've dealt with angels before, Cassiel. Fallen and otherwise. I knew what you were when we met. I could smell it on you. Plus, you have to be the real deal. Only an actual angel can annoy me this much." He puffed away at his cigarette, clicking his pen again and jotting notes into his book. "I had to push. I needed to make sure you weren't on the edge of the abyss. You don't seem to be if you can still call up that much holy fire, so that leaves me in the uncomfortable position of having to take the job." He sighed heavily, and that tiredness he had exuded since I'd arrived seemed to deepen.

"I feel like I've missed something," I said, sinking back into the chair and staring at him.

For the first time since we'd met, Axton smiled at me, the cigarette filter clenched in his teeth. While it was a genuine expression, there was some fierceness in his eyes I didn't entirely understand. "I'm okay with that."

He didn't explain, and he looked back at the notepad as he wrote. "I didn't lie about not seeing eye-to-eye with God. Or the church. We don't get along and haven't in a few hundred years, at least. But if this really is one of the actual nails, I can't just ignore it. Something like that could hurt a whole lotta people who don't deserve it. I was around for the Crusades and saw what relics did on the battlefield." He went quiet for a moment, looking past me and at the wall as though lost in a memory. Axton's attention returned to the present with a growl. "Much as I don't like it, I can't stand by and watch." His lips twisted in an annoyed expression as though he had eaten something bitter.

I rubbed a hand over my face. I had gone from wanting to strangle him to a sense of intense relief in the span of a few minutes, and the whiplash of emotions exhausted me.

Either ignoring my turmoil or finding some sense of amusement in it, Axton smirked. "You want some coffee?"

"Uh, sure." The question felt unusually mundane against the backdrop of the conversation we'd just been having.

Axton stood up and ambled over to the coffee maker with his gigantic mug.

"What are you?" I asked, craning my head around to look at him. "I could feel you absorbing my Grace."

He grunted. "Something old enough to know the kind of trouble this is, and that if angels are involved, shit's going to go bad in a hurry."

That didn't answer my question, but I got the feeling pushing wouldn't get me more answers. "All right." I sighed and tried to let go of the anger I was still carrying while Axton fussed with the coffee.

It took him three or four runs to get enough coffee in his mug. He then made a cup for me, bringing over the packets of sugar and cup of individually packaged cream. Axton set all of that on the desk before returning to his chair and reaching down beside him to pull up a bottle of creamer from somewhere and dumping a considerable amount into his cup, stirring with a finger until he was satisfied with the color. After replacing the creamer from wherever he'd gotten it from, he picked up the cup and drank for a long time in silence.

I added cream and sugar to my coffee while he downed his. "So where does that leave us?" I asked.

"That," he said, "is a damn good question."

# CHAPTER 13

A xton spent the next hour or so picking my brain. I told him about the demon, what I'd learned, what my brother had said, and everything else I could think of relating to the case. He also asked me, in detail, everything I knew about the demon that had killed Father John, just in case the two events were related somehow. While there was no obvious tie between them, I wasn't entirely certain why the first demon had killed Father John. All the demonic activity could be connected for all we knew.

I left his office around two in the afternoon, hungry and exhausted. While I wasn't exactly welcome in the church when not at work, I still had a key to the door into the kitchen and knew Dust kept sandwich supplies there. This time of day, the kitchen would be empty anyway, and I could probably sneak in without getting myself noticed. That, and I had volunteered enough hours over the last two years to have earned myself the right to a modest lunch.

The flight to the church wasn't far, and while my back still ached from the healing injuries to it, I much preferred flying to walking. When I walked, all the streets looked the same in some parts of the city, and it was far easier to get lost. From the air, I knew what landmarks to look for and couldn't take a wrong turn down a side street somewhere.

Fifteen or so minutes later, I landed in the courtyard at the church and banished my wings, sagging a little with fatigue. The flight had taken more out of me than I expected, and my stomach's need for food had progressed from a polite request to an imperious demand. I walked to the kitchen and unlocked the door, heading inside.

The nerve center of the St. Mary's soup kitchen resembled an industrial kitchen in a restaurant with a number of stainless steel prep tables lining the center, cooking surfaces along one wall, and several deep sinks and a massive refrigerator along another. Dry goods were kept in a pantry off to the side. It received regular donations from local grocery stores, the occasional bakery, and of course parishioners who gave what they could. I had spent a great deal of time there and found it soothing, even with the lights off in the quiet of a winter afternoon. Maybe especially so since the buzz of the fluorescents were grating when they were on.

Working in the soup kitchen had been one of the first things Father John encouraged me to do, and it had been where I'd met Dust. I was no great cook, but Dust had taught me how to pare vegetables, wash dishes, mash potatoes, and so on. I couldn't make much of a meal from start to finish, but I could help someone else do it without cutting myself or destroying anything. Most of the time.

Of all the jobs I'd done in that kitchen, the knife work was the most comfortable since I had been created with an innate knowledge of weaponry. I could pick up any weapon and understand it and know how to utilize it. That included, much to Jim's surprise, firearms. I could field strip a firearm of any type in seconds with my eyes closed and reassemble it just as quickly. The first few times I'd done it in front of any of my friends, they'd been incredulous. Particularly since I sometimes had issues navigating my cell phone menus.

While I was poking around in the refrigerator to collect the cold cuts, mayonnaise, and hunting for the mustard for my sandwich, a voice made me jump so suddenly, I bashed my head off the door.

"Angel, tell me, is this the only mustard you have? It is just deplorable."

I spun around, rubbing the back of my head, to see Asakku sitting on one of the preparation tables with a sandwich, the mustard I'd been looking for on the table next to him. He wore yet another different suit to the last one I'd seen, but it still retained the black and red motif. His handsome face was screwed up in displeasure, and he scowled at the sandwich in his hands as though it had personally offended him. Dust made that face once when I mixed up cumin and cinnamon in the spice cupboard once, and he ended up spicing a batch of chili with it.

"There are other kinds of mustard?" I asked, dumbfounded. His presence confused me, but the mustard situation struck me as too ridiculous for the rest of the questions I could have—and should have—been asking to come to the forefront.

"Oh, you poor, neglected, sheltered being." He shook his head and took another bite of his sandwich.

"If it is so awful, why are you still eating it?" I asked, trying to ignore him and assembling my own lunch on another table. I could do without mustard.

"Gluttony."

An abrupt laugh left me before I could stop it. Which turned into a scowl. I had no business laughing at a demon's jokes.

He grinned, slid off the table, and walked closer to me, leaning his hands on the surface I was working at. I could feel his eyes on me. "You look much improved from the last time I saw you."

"I am. Thanks to you." I didn't like acknowledging that, but it was the truth, and I thought, perhaps, if I humored him, he would give me more information about my objective. While I have never been skilled in subversion, I know enough about tactics to understand buttering someone up a little. Plus, if there's one thing to know about demons, it's that their ego is always the way to whatever they have that resembles a heart. Stroke it, and they purr. Poke it too hard, and it infuriates them beyond sense.

Asakku smiled, revealing even, white teeth. "Indeed. How is your hunt for the nail going?" Whether it was my feeding his ego or he was amused at my expense for some reason, his expression appeared satisfied.

I shrugged, trying to keep my manner casual. "It has barely started. I am not even certain where to look in the city for such a thing, let alone how to acquire it."

"Perhaps you should pray for guidance," he suggested. "He might throw you a bone."

"I am not a dog."

"And yet you were kept on so short a leash that one little mistake and," he waggled his fingers, "poof! You're down here in the dirt with the rest of us."

I stiffened, gripping the plastic knife I was using to spread mayonnaise and pointing it at him. "That was my mistake, and I do not blame the Father for that." Despite knowing he was, of course, trying to get exactly that reaction, I couldn't stop my anger. There were a few topics that never failed to get under my skin, and my fall was one of them.

Asakku held up his hands in a placating gesture and straightened, his expression unfazed. Then again, I was threatening him with a plastic butter knife, so I suppose I wasn't at my most intimidating. "Oh, she bites. Bad doggie. I would not be what I am if I did not, *mn,*" he made a little grunting noise, "push." The grin faltered when he mentioned his nature, twisting into a sneer. Though it didn't feel like it was directed at me.

I finished assembling my sandwich and put everything I'd used back where it belonged, taking deep breaths and going over all the reasons I shouldn't start a fight at that exact moment. When I looked back, he was sitting where he had been when I'd walked in, though there was no more sandwich. Either he'd finished it or... honestly, I had no idea.

Some demons have the power to twist reality ever so slightly. Make you see things or sometimes even make very real things work in slightly strange ways. It's somewhat like fae illusions, though not quite. More subtle than that. Usually, these little ripples and twists seem or feel entirely real to the person — or people — they are meant for. Some can even do very real damage with such conjurations. When an angel, or say, the Son of Man, does such a thing, it's a miracle (I refer you to the loaves and fishes situation). When a demon does it, it's usually to tempt or torment.

However, I couldn't imagine him using such power to create a sandwich. After all, who warps the threads of reality to conjure a sandwich into existence just to complain about the mustard?

"We could make a game of this," Asakku said, his smile returning as he sat on the table again, his legs crossed at the ankle and hands laced together behind his head.

"Of what?" I asked, sighing and taking a bite of my sandwich. At that point, I couldn't be sure if my irritation was his fault or the product of my hunger. I could solve exactly one of those problems in that moment, so I went with what I had.

He rolled his eyes and lolled his head to the side to stare at me as though I were the dumbest person on the planet. "The nail. We could play... Oh, what is that game the children play. Hot and Cold, maybe?"

My frustration continued to simmer, but I did my best to keep my tone light, though I couldn't quite keep it out of my voice. "And if I'm not in a playful mood?"

"*You* might not be, but *I* am, which is what matters here, dear angel." Asakku's grin was toothy as he leaned toward me, emberlike eyes glowing faintly. "Shall we play?" I didn't trust that expression. Of course, I didn't trust any expression he made. Or his face in general.

"What is Hot and Cold?" I asked, trying to humor him at least a little. Angering him seemed unproductive, and I couldn't fight an archdemon *and* eat a sandwich at the same time. I'm good, but I'm not that good.

"Oh, it is an old game the mortals played. Basically, one person hides an object, and the others seek it. The person hiding it tells the seekers when they are close or far away. When they are cold or..." Suddenly he was there, pressed up against my back, his hands covering mine on the table. Asakku leaned in close, his mouth almost to my ear, the heat of his body radiating against my skin even through my clothes. "...hot."

I balked and shoved away. My back ached when I did, and I grunted, facing him again but creating distance between us. My heart beat a little harder in my chest, and I had to catch my breath before I could answer. "And what, exactly, are you hiding?"

"We were talking about an ancient relic. You know, the power to shape creation? Keep up, angel." Asakku smirked, crossing his arms as though my retreat had been some kind of victory for him.

My mind rebooted a little. "You know where the nail is?"

"I couldn't very well play if I didn't."

"Why not just tell me if you want me to find it so badly?" I took another bite of my sandwich, suppressing the desire to punch his smiling teeth in.

He waved a hand dismissively and sniffed. "Because then it wouldn't be much of a *game* now, would it? When you've been here as long as I have, you get bored, dear angel."

"Stop calling me that," I snapped, glowering at him, my patience hitting its limits.

The smile in his eyes with just a hint of triumph told me that was exactly the reaction he was hoping for. "Never."

I stuffed the last of the sandwich in my mouth and chewed to prevent myself from saying something both inappropriate for church and unbecoming for an angel of the Lord. The time it took me to chew the wad of lunchmeat, cheese, and bread allowed me to take a mental breather. If he wanted me to find this artifact, it had to be part of some bigger scheme of his. But if I got my hands on it, there was a good chance I could keep it away from him. Something like that would be fueled by Grace. I doubted he could even touch it without suffering severe injury, but that didn't mean he couldn't use it for *something*. If I got to it before his game finished — whatever his intentions — I had a good chance of circumventing whatever plans he'd made. Either that, or the whole thing was a trap.

It was probably a trap.

Regardless, there wasn't much I could do about it. Ignoring the nail's presence and refusing could unleash a devastating power on the world. Playing his game was a risk. I had no idea what his scheme was, and he was already twelve steps ahead of me playing a chess game I couldn't see the full board of.

I swallowed. "Fine. I'll play."

He clapped with the giddy pleasure of a child. "Delightful! I will be in touch. For now," he glanced toward the door as though seeing or hearing something that didn't make itself known to me, "I have matters to tend to. Though rest assured, I will be watching your progress with great interest."

"Wait, am I hot or cold right now?" I asked, unsure exactly what the rules of the game were.

In the blink of an eye, Asakku was across the space between us, standing against me, crowding me into the refrigerator. "You, dear angel, are," he drew a hissing breath in through his teeth, "very, very hot. But in terms of the game? Cold. Frigid, even."

I didn't know how to respond and blushed, which seemed to amuse him, and he pulled away. "Be safe out there, Cassiel, angel of the Lord." He left through the back door of the kitchen without looking back.

# CHAPTER 14

D ust had given me a business card with a phone number on it written in dark blue ballpoint pen. It read, "T's Repairs and Service" with a pair of crossed wrenches. Below that was an address with a business phone number and an email. The back was blank but for the phone number (separate from the business line) he'd written on it for me.

It took me a few minutes to put my head together after Asakku left, but when I had, I dialed the number. It rang a few times, but a deep, gruff voice answered. "This is T."

"Oh, ah," I stammered, abruptly nervous. "My name is Cass. Dust told me—"

"Yep. Was expecting your call. He said you were looking for work, right?"

"Yes, but—"

"I know, no ID. You anywhere near the shop?"

"I have no idea, honestly. I don't know where your shop is. I have the address, but—"

"All right. Where are you, then?"

I told him the address of the church, and I could hear the keys of a computer keyboard clacking in the background. "About two and half miles as the fae fly. Could take the T or fly. If you fly. You got wings? Or I could come get you."

"I have wings," I said, not wanting him to go out of his way for me. Besides, he was probably at work, and I understood that leaving work midday wasn't good outside of an emergency. Of course, I had already flown up to the center of the city and back. The wounds across my back warned me going further wouldn't be the best decision I had made that day. Then again, I had agreed to play games with a demon, so what was another poor life choice?

"All right." He gave me some landmarks to look for from the air and told me to head northeast from the church, following Blue Hill Ave until it intersected with

Cottage Street. Then follow Cottage Street to Norfolk Ave. I listened, told him I would do my best, and then we rang off.

I cleaned up the kitchen, not that I'd left much of a mess. I did, however, spend some extra time scrubbing down the prep table Asakku had sat on. It wasn't as though he'd left any marks or dirt, but anything he'd touched just struck me as unclean somehow. Outside, I took to the air and followed T's directions.

With the number of flying creatures in the world, the names of larger roads are painted on the surface to be visible from the air. While a lot of us use GPS to get around, those without find the painted signs easier than "near the big building that looks like every other building around it but with cars." Some businesses even have signage or their names painted on the roof that allow quick identification from above.

Once in the air, I turned north, following the directions I'd been given. While I could walk, I vastly preferred flight even to driving. It took fifteen or twenty minutes for Jim to navigate traffic to get to the church from his home. It took me less than half that time unless there was bad weather or I was particularly exhausted or injured. While there were certainly other fliers in the sky, we had the benefit of not dealing with traffic signals or road congestion. It was easy enough to avoid one another if one were paying attention. Particularly since we can move in three dimensions. In winter, there were far fewer people in the skies than in the warmer months, also. Getting above the buildings made for a windier and colder journey, even if it was faster.

I arrived at a building with a sign matching the business card in less than ten minutes and looked around. The squat brick building had three closed bay doors with an office on the left side. A sign on the door proclaimed it open, and when I opened the door, a doorbell-like sound came from the shop.

"Be with you in a minute!" I recognized T's voice from the phone when he called out from deeper in the building, raised to cut through the sounds of work through the doorway into the shop floor.

The waiting room had a collection of chairs designed for larger occupants than most places, and a broad plate glass window let the meager winter sun into the space. A coffee table showed recent issues of multiple magazines ranging from *Vanity Fair* and *Newsweek* to several in languages I didn't recognize, though the orcs, elves, dwarves, and so on displayed on the front covers gave me some hint to who they were meant for. Against the wall was a little coffee bar with a single-serving coffee maker, single-serve cups, and an assortment of creamers and such. It struck me that most offices must have those things since I'd also seen one in Axton's a few hours earlier.

While the trappings differed, the waiting room here and the one at Axton's agency looked very similar to one another. Except this one had matching furniture and no fountain.

A few minutes later, an ogre wearing blue-gray coveralls emerged from the shop, wiping his hands on a shop towel. Unlike Dust, who was a mottled gray, T was greenish-gray in color. Almost the color of the olive drab pants Jim often wore. He was also quite a bit bigger than Dust, being nearly a foot taller—virtues of him being an ogre to Dust's orcish nature. One of his tusks was broken down to the line of his lips, which gave him a bit of an awkward smile, but his dark brown eyes were warm and friendly. "You must be Cass," he said, rounding the counter and approaching me with a hand extended.

Of the three "tusked" races—orcs, ogres, and trolls—ogres are the mid-size and tend to be around seven feet tall. The three races share ancestry and have a great deal of close genetic makeup. They're typically grouped together due to their similarity in appearance, shared language, and cultural similarities, but there are enough differences to make them distinct. Also, scientifically speaking, they're separate, though I couldn't tell you how exactly.

I stood and shook his hand, finding his grip warm and surprisingly gentle for someone his size and with the amount of muscle he carried. I had expected a crushing handshake. Instead, it was firm enough to be confident, but he was obviously accustomed to taking care with those who had smaller hands than he did. "Dust said you might be willing to help me find work."

"Yeah. He told me he had someone who needed help. You ever work on a car?"

I shook my head, steeling myself for rejection. My gaze lowered, my shoulders lifting. I wished they wouldn't because I knew my body language betrayed just how uncomfortable and uncertain I felt. "Fake it 'til you make it," was what Eirlas had told me when I was first learning to interact with people. Feigning confidence and just going for it was not, however, among the things I was good at. Faking anything was hard for me. Well, outside of feints in combat, but that's a completely different subject.

However, T gave me a considering look without judgment. "All right. You ever work a counter?"

I shook my head again, the feeling of anxiety crawling up my ribs into my heart. The base, primal part of my mind told me to run, but I ignored it.

"Have any experience on the phones, then?"

The awkward, apologetic smile on my face must've told him everything he needed to know. But instead of telling me to get out or even politely asking me to leave, he shrugged and pointed to the sitting area. "All right, well, let's start with this, then." He gestured to me to sit down again, and he flopped into one of the chairs nearby. "How are you with people?"

I sat, looking at the floor and picking at the sleeve of my shirt. "I am... uncomfortable with them. Awkward. I don't always know what to say, and..." I trailed off, feeling somewhat ashamed. Here I was with Dust having vouched for me, and I couldn't do anything this man needed.

"Then we'll get you started with changing oil and helping me keep the shop clean. I'll teach you the rest as we go. With you being one of Dust's friends from the church, I gotta ask. Where are you staying?"

The answer surprised me, and I lifted my head, meeting his eyes for a second. The question he'd asked registered in my brain, and I rubbed the back of my neck and looked down again, trying to formulate an answer.

"It's like that, is it?" His voice softened. "Not that it's any of my business, 'cause it's not, but if you need a place to crash, my guest room is always open."

"You don't even know me."

"'I was hungry, and you gave me something to eat. I was thirsty, and you gave me something to drink. I was a stranger, and you invited me in.' It's fine. That's what we do." He reached up to the neck of his coveralls and pulled out a cross on a thick golden chain. It looked proportionate around his neck, but for anyone else, it would have been gigantic. "We're supposed to take care of each other. If Dust sent you to me, that means he trusts you. If he trusts you — thinks you're good people — then so do I."

"What about... Isn't it trouble if I stay and I'm not on the..." I couldn't remember the word. The anxiety was giving way to something worse: hope. Anxiety, I could handle. Hope was an emotion I had mixed feelings toward because, on one hand, it meant the possibility of brighter things. On the other hand, it wasn't a certainty, so relying on it felt thin.

"Pah. My landlord doesn't give a shit about that kind of thing." T waved a hand dismissively. "My neighbors don't say anything about who I have staying with me. I don't say anything about who they have staying with them. We've got an understanding."

Indecision welled up in me. I had barely met the man, and he was offering me work and a place to stay. It was almost too much. I swallowed hard and nodded, looking at the floor.

"Listen, Cass," he said in his deep rumble of a voice, "you don't need to answer now. Me'n my shop? We're not going anywhere. If you need some time to think things over and make a choice, that's fine. I don't need an answer now." He spoke the words softly, his manner unlike any military man I'd met. It was no wonder he and Dust were friends.

Jim and Dust were kind, and I loved them. They loved me. But both of them tended to be a little harder edged. Not that Jim didn't know how to be gentle, and he was good at it. There was something different about T, though. Some kind of softness or tenderness of spirit I hadn't experienced since Father John.

"If I work, it will help to cover the costs of me staying with you, correct?" My voice shook a little.

T grunted. "You can look at it that way if you want, but I'm still going to pay you."

"Where do you live?"

"Neponset. It's about two miles from here. Mile and a half from the church."

"I would not be in the way?"

"I have an extra bedroom I'm not even using. If you decide to stay for longer'n a few nights, it's yours, but let's take this a few days at a time for now. You don't need to commit to anything just yet. Let me show you the shop, show you some of the work, and you can decide if you wanna do it." His awkward, cockeyed smile reassured me.

If I did decide to move, what about Maggie and Ether? Would I see them again? Not that, I supposed, we were really friends. We slept in the same space was all.

Looked out for each other. Would one of them benefit from this opportunity more?

T rose and closed the distance between us to put his hand on my shoulder, which dragged me out of my thoughts. "C'mon." He patted me a couple times, the contact firm enough to drive the air out of my lungs, and then lumbered out toward the shop ahead of me.

I stood and followed him into the shop, studying the layout. T's garage had three bays with lifts in each, and a long workbench with a couple stools at different locations. Devices sat on the workbench along with an array of parts scattered across the work surface. One of the lifts had a car on it with a light hanging from the bottom of the frame. It smelled a little like gasoline and engine oil in there, but not so strongly that it suggested a spill. Just a general scent of engines and work that I would come to understand as being part of life in a shop.

In addition, the faint scent of tobacco trailed in the air, though I couldn't identify what kind. It smelled different from the cigarettes I'd been around, and even from the strange black ones Axton had been smoking. It was thicker, somehow, and very pungent.

At the time, I knew nothing about cars and less about shops and had never even been in one. I knew the pedals made you go faster or slower (or a lever in the case of Jim's van), and the steering wheel controlled direction somehow, but that was the extent of it.

T showed me around, helping me find everything. The sheer number of tools and devices in there intimidated me since I had no understanding of how any of them worked. But when I said so to T, he laughed.

"You'll only need to worry about a very few of 'em for a long while, Cass. Changing oil's easy. I'll show you every step of the way, and you'll figure it out in no time. Don't worry. Most of this," he gestured around to the various tools, "is for jobs you won't need to worry about for a long while, if ever. Or they're tools that all do the same thing at different sizes. Like these." He pulled open a drawer of his toolbox to show me several rows of wrenches. "You see these? They all do the exact same thing, just different sizes." He pulled out a small one and then a much larger one. "They still just turn nuts. Some of the other tools I have do exactly the same thing but at different angles or hold onto 'em differently. It's not as bad as it looks. You just gotta know which tool does which job." He put the wrenches down in their places again, adjusting them a little until they were just so and then closed the drawer again.

His no-nonsense explanation made sense to me, and I smiled, reassured at the notion that perhaps they weren't unbearably complex after all. It was still a lot, but knowing he didn't expect me to learn the intricacies immediately went a long way toward soothing my worries.

We spent the rest of the afternoon in there with T letting me shadow him while he worked. He even taught me how to change the oil on one of the cars he had. I wound up covered in it, much to his amusement. Rather than be angry at the mess, he helped me clean it up, had me change out of the borrowed coveralls and into a clean set, and had me get right back to it. He proved to be a patient teacher and seemed unbothered by the endless questions I asked him about parts of the engine and how they worked.

# CHAPTER 15

"It's about time to close," T said, distracting me from my work on changing some engine oil. I'd figured it out pretty quickly, and after my first oil bath, I'd avoided taking another.

"Close?" I looked at the clock and did a double take. I had been there a good four hours. "Oh. I'm sorry, I didn't—"

"Sorry? You helped." T grinned. "You're fine. But you should decide if you're staying with me for the night or not. If you don't want to, I can drop you off wherever you like." He patted my back as he passed, his large hand thumping between my shoulder blades.

I sucked in a breath and grimaced as he struck one of the still-healing injuries, and he froze. "I'm sorry. Didn't know you were hurt. You okay?" He frowned, his eyes worried and apologetic.

"Healing," I grated, shaking my head. "It's all right."

"Still. Should'a been more careful." He sighed. "You sure you should be sleeping rough in this cold if you're injured?"

He reminded me of Jim, always pestering me. It annoyed me a little, but at the same time, I knew his heart was in the right place. And he wasn't entirely wrong. "It is more comfortable to sleep somewhere warmer while I'm recovering," I admitted, closing the hood of the car I'd been working on and grabbing the shop towel I had nearby to wipe my hands off.

T nodded and stripped off his coveralls, revealing a set of jeans and a long-sleeved flannel beneath them. "I believe it. So that settles it for tonight, then—you're staying with me." He tossed the coveralls into the laundry bin he'd shown me when I'd drenched myself in oil the first time before making his way out front for a moment, then carried the cash drawer into his office.

The shop office was off the main floor of the shop adjacent to the waiting area, though the door was accessible through the shop itself. T lumbered inside and rounded a desk, sinking into the chair that creaked in protest before he started counting the money in the register and typing into the computer he had there. A pair of too-small half moon reading glasses sat at the end of his nose, and he squinted through them at the screen. The effect struck me as comical, and I smiled involuntarily. The only other people I'd seen with glasses like that were the older women at the church, so they seemed incredibly out of place on T's broad, tusked face with his large, flat nose.

I stripped off my coveralls and put them into the laundry bin just like he had and washed my hands with some gritty, orange-smelling soap from a violently orange pump bottle he had sitting beside a sink. To my surprise, it removed the grime on my skin with little effort and left them smelling pleasant. I wondered if we should get a bottle of it for some of the cleaning work we did in the church kitchen.

By the time I'd finished washing up, T had emerged from the office. He offered me several folded bills. "Here."

Unable to understand why he was handing me money, I accepted them on reflex. "I… Thank you? What is this for?"

"You worked, didn't you? Deserve to be paid for it." He smiled at me. "It's not much, but you were only here a few hours. If you start working full days, it'll be more."

I stared at the money in my hand, frowning. It felt strange. While Jim, Dust, and Eirlas had given me money before to help me survive, I hadn't really earned it like this. Without counting it — it seemed like it would be rude — I pulled out my wallet and put the bills in it. My wallet usually didn't have much of anything in it, but Jim had said I should get used to carrying one just in case. Plus, I kept a spare key to the church in there. "Oh. I… guess I wasn't thinking about that."

"I can tell. All you were thinking about was the work." T grinned. "Did you decide where you wanted me to take you?" His words were at odds with his earlier proclamation that I was staying with him, but he obviously wanted to give me a choice in the matter. Sort of.

"If you don't mind, I think I would find it helpful to sleep inside tonight. But my things are at Jim's house."

T nodded. "If you give me his address, I'll take you there so you can pick them up. We can get dinner on the way."

When he mentioned food, my stomach reminded me I hadn't eaten since around noon, and then I'd only had a sandwich. "I can pay for it. I have money."

T shook his head. "Nah. My treat. I'll finish locking up, then we can get outta here." He passed me and walked out front, locking the door and turning the sign from "open" to "closed." He then shut off the sign near the road using a switch on the wall and returned to the shop, turning off the lights in the waiting area and closing (and locking) the door between the shop and the waiting rooms. He did the same with the office before shooing me out a door in the back wall of the shop and locking the outer door.

Behind the business was a small, fenced-in parking lot with several cars in it. T led me to a large truck—very similar to Dust's—and we climbed in. The truck looked older than some of the models I'd seen on the road, but he'd kept it in impeccable condition. No rust, and the interior was immaculate. He fired it up, and the engine rumbled quietly like an oversized cat. T patted the dashboard. "So, where we goin'?"

I gave him Jim's address and texted Jim to let him know I was staying at T's that night and we were coming by for my things. He replied with an assent.

---

When we arrived at Jim's after stopping for fast food, I climbed out of the truck and told T that I would be back shortly. I then headed inside, where Jim let me into his apartment with a smile.

"Hey. Went well, I take it?" he asked.

"Yes. I think it is work I can learn to do." Despite being sore and exhausted, I felt triumphant somehow. "T is a very kind man, and he works very hard. I think... I think we can be friends." I stepped further in to let Jim close the door to the chill in the hallway.

Jim smiled, his expression relieved. His shoulders sagged a little with the release of tension I hadn't realized he was carrying. "Good. I've been praying that we'd find a way to get you a place to live. He's letting you stay with him?"

"He offered to let me stay the night but said I can stay longer if I need to. He has an arrangement with his neighbors." I walked around to the couch and put my few belongings into my backpack, picking it up. "He even paid me for my work today." I produced my wallet and showed Jim the cash. All in all, it was about fifty bucks, which was a small fortune to me at the time. I'd never had so much money at once.

"That's wonderful, Cass. Good job." Jim rolled over and took my hand, squeezing it firmly with a brilliant smile. "I hope this is the start of a new chapter in your life. Maybe one with more nights spent indoors. Normally, I'd be skeptical about you staying with a stranger, but since he's one of Dust's friends, I'm less concerned."

I squeezed his fingers back and then leaned down to hug him. "Thank you."

"Stop acting like this is goodbye, you idiot," he said with a laugh. "You still have to come to the church to volunteer. It's not like anything is going to change."

"If I am working, then..."

"The shop probably closes at, what, five?"

"That was when he said we were done."

"Dinner service doesn't start until seven, and my groups run at eight. So you'd best get your holy hiney to the church to help." He pointed at me menacingly, though his eyes glittered with good humor.

"Yes, sir!" I said, straightening and giving him a facsimile of a salute.

"At ease," Jim answered, laughing. "Go on. I'll see you soon."

I nodded and carried my bag out, though when I got to the curb, I paused, looking toward the bridge. It felt strange to leave the people there and say nothing. Frowning, I walked up to T's truck and opened the passenger door, putting my backpack and bedroll on the floor there. "May I have a minute?"

T glanced at the clock. "I got time. Everything okay?"

"Yes. I just wanted to let some people know I won't be there tonight. I don't want them to worry." The contractions still felt strange to say, but I was trying to use them more often.

He nodded. "All right. I'll be here."

I smiled a little to him and took off toward the bridge at a jog. It was only a couple blocks anyway. As I ran, I considered the changes in my state of affairs and sent up a prayer of thanks. Without a doubt, there had been divine intervention to get me a place to stay just as I needed it. Having a place to stay and a job would mean I could earn money. That money I could use to take care of my needs and then maybe even repay some of the kindness shown to me.

Speaking of kindness, when I arrived under the bridge, Ether and Maggie were huddled around the usual small bit of flame Maggie conjured for them. Both looked up at me and nodded in greeting. Maggie smiled. Ether didn't, but she rarely smiled anyway.

"I have found work," I told them, unable to contain my excitement. "And my employer is allowing me to stay with him."

Maggie grinned, but Ether's reaction was more cautious. "What kind of work, Cass?" She spoke slowly, gaze serious and concerned.

"I am working at a car repair shop. The owner is friends with Dust, my friend from the church."

She relaxed a little, the tension draining from her. I realized, then, that she had worried someone was taking advantage of me. My heart warmed at her desire to protect me. "Oh, well, that's great news, then." A faint ghost of a smile turned the corner of her mouth up. It was about the best she ever did. "Good for you. Why are you down here, then?"

The question gave me pause. "I, uh, just thought I'd tell you so you didn't worry when I stopped coming here at night."

Ether nodded. "Ah, okay. Well, message received. I'm happy for you. Truly."

Maggie jumped up and ran over to hug me. "I'm happy for you, too. That's fantastic news." She wrapped her arms around my neck, making me hunch down a little to return the hug. "God is good!"

"He is indeed." I extricated myself from the hug. Hunching like that made the still-healing wounds burn. On impulse, I looked between them. "Listen, I got paid today. I will be working more tomorrow." I pulled out my wallet and took the money T had given me, offering it to the two women. "This should help you."

When I held the cash out toward them, Maggie shook her head. "Oh, Cass, you should keep that. You earned it."

"I have a place to sleep and a job now. You need this more than I do."

When Maggie hedged, Ether took the money and pocketed it. "I'll make sure we get something useful with it. Maybe get everyone some food or something. Thanks."

That wan smile of hers returned for a moment before vanishing. I knew she'd use it for the good of the group and trusted her to make sure it went where it was needed most.

I returned my wallet to my pocket. "I should go. My employer is waiting for me."

"Take care of yourself," Ether said with a nod.

"Don't forget us," Maggie chirped before she crouched near the fire again, warming her hands.

"I will not forget you." The idea hurt somehow. How could I forget them? They had helped me. Befriended me. I couldn't just forget them. Though, realistically, I doubted how often I would see them given everything going on.

After our goodbyes, I made my way back to where T was waiting, listening to the radio as his truck idled at the curb. When I climbed in, he smiled. "Ready?"

I nodded. "Yes."

T put the truck in gear, and we rumbled off into the rush hour traffic.

# CHAPTER 16

T's apartment sat on the third floor of a square brick building with no elevator. He fussed with the door for a minute, grumbling about needing to put some graphite in the lock, before letting us into his space. The two-bedroom apartment was bright and as spotless as the interior of his car. We entered a short hallway, and T told me to take off my shoes and put them on a mat near the door so as to not track mud and dirt inside. He did the same, then led me into the living space of his apartment in his stocking feet. Beside the large set of work boots he wore, my shoes looked almost like a child's.

The first thing I noticed was a massive, shaggy, gray-furred dog barreling at me. He reared up on his hind legs, draped his paws over my shoulders, and licked my face until T pushed him away. His name must have been a joke because on his hind legs, he was easily my height. I had almost no experience with animals, but I knew instantly I liked this one. I had seen dogs on my walks but had never interacted with one and wondered if they were all so delightful.

"Sorry. That's Tiny. He's harmless; he just likes to lick people to death. I should've warned you." T gave me an apologetic smile as he gave the beast several heavy thumps to the ribs.

I patted the dog's head and received more licks to my fingers as I did so. "I like him." I had seen dogs lick people as a sign of affection both on television and in the world, so I understood that much. "He's very friendly."

"Well, he sure likes you back. Got him years ago as a guard dog, but you can see how well that went. If he could, he'd invite people in so long as they rub his belly." T rolled his eyes but scratched the dog's ears with familiar affection while he complained.

Ogre-sized furniture crammed the living room in what I imagined felt like a rather cramped space to T, given his size. A couch, easy chair, television set, coffee table, and a dining set took up most of the floor space. It looked like the table and chairs were mostly kept out of the way, so I suspected he typically used them for guests rather than himself. T headed into the kitchen, adjacent to the living room.

"You want a beer?" he offered as he stared into the refrigerator.

The kitchen had a half wall between the spaces with the expected amenities. A small—by ogre standards—table sat in a corner by the window with a single chair at it. Something about that struck me as a little lonely, though T seemed happy enough so far as I could tell.

"No thank you." I had tried beer once, but I didn't enjoy the flavor much. Father John had told me it was an acquired taste, but I had no idea why anyone would want to acquire it. Coupled with the fact that alcohol, along with all medications I'd ever encountered, had absolutely no effect on me, I had no interest in the stuff whatsoever.

I sat on the couch, finding it far softer than I had expected and, being ogre-sized, I felt an odd sense of displacement. Like I were small and the world was gigantic. Tiny leapt up next to me and lay his huge head in my lap, demanding further attention. I gladly provided it, finding his incessant need to be touched a pleasant diversion from my awkwardness.

T came out of the kitchen and flopped into the chair, turning on the television. "The bathroom's down there," he said, pointing down a hallway to his right. "Door in the middle on the left. You can use the soap in there if you want to take a shower."

"Thank you." I smiled, the awkward uncertainty returning. Not sure what to do with myself, my leg started bouncing as if possessing a mind of its own. "How much time do you expect me to work tomorrow?"

"Well, that's up to you." He leaned forward in his chair, resting his elbows on his knees. If he noticed my discomfort, he didn't speak on it. "You got things going on?"

"I might. I am working with a private investigator to find something important." I didn't want to tell him about everything, but informing him that my time might be spoken for seemed prudent.

"Ah, in that case, you can work unless he calls and says he needs something. I head in for nine a.m. and close around five. If you're coming in with me in the morning, I can give you a ride."

"Thank you." I smiled, giving him a sidelong look. "Does that count as taking the T to work?"

He burst out laughing. "Oh, you have a sense of humor?" he asked, grin teasing. "I was beginning to worry. You're so serious and wound up all the time."

I smiled. "I'm not very good at jokes, but I do enjoy them." The anxiety eased some with his amusement and teasing, and my shoulders relaxed a little.

We spent the rest of the evening chatting and watching the news. It was a strangely comfortable thing, not too dissimilar from spending time with Jim. The two were somewhat similar in attitude, though T had a manner to him I could only describe as paternal. He offered to wash my clothes for me and loaned me one of his shirts while he did. That came with clucking over the fact that the shirt had oil stains on the cuff and grumbling about how they were never going to come out. It was strange to be fussed over in such a way. Not that Jim didn't take good care of me as his guest when I was there, but T treated me almost as though I were one of his children.

I learned, through the course of our conversation, T had three children: Torook, Ingrid, and Brekur. He spoke with great pride about them, becoming animated and heaping glowing praise upon all three in turn. Ingrid was a lawyer specializing in representing the tusked races in civil rights cases in Canada. She had a husband of her own and several children. Torook, also, had taken a career path not traditional for the tusked races, who were typically relegated to blue collar jobs. Torook taught history at Harvard. Brekur, on the other hand, much preferred working with his hands and was a foreman for a construction company in Connecticut. He was the youngest, and Tremor fretted about him some since he had a bit of a temper.

T didn't see his children often, but they all came home for Christmas every year. He took out his phone and showed me pictures of his family, extolling their many virtues and accomplishments. It was strange to be around since none of the people in my life had such families. Jim had never mentioned any family members in my time knowing him. Nor had Dust or Eirlas. I assumed they either were estranged or didn't have any living family, but I'd never thought it right to ask them about it since they didn't bring it up. The only person whose family I had met was Mary Beth, a girl who had been swept up in the demon business of the past autumn. While she was all right now, my brief encounter with her father had ended with me breaking his nose.

In my defense, he deserved it.

By the end of the evening, I had showered and was wearing one of T's t-shirts. This led me to joke about how Boston must be a "T town," which inspired T to tell me about the Boston Tea Party, which led to further jokes of the same caliber. T had my clothes in the laundry to make sure I had clean garments to wear for the next day. The shirt he loaned me fell to my calves. The neck was large enough that it hung off one of my shoulders, which felt awkward, but T didn't appear to have noticed.

"I can take you to Walmart to get some more clothes if you need 'em," he offered as he returned my clothing to me, now dry and smelling like laundry soap.

I shook my head. "I don't have any money."

He raised a brow, expression perplexed. "I just paid you. Or I meant to. I thought I had." He reached for his wallet.

I forestalled him by holding up a hand. "I gave it to the people under the bridge. I had been staying with them, and they need it more. I can earn more money tomorrow."

T smiled and nodded, wrinkles around his eyes crinkling. It reminded me a little of Father John. "Giving your last coin is more valuable than giving in abundance if you're rich. I get it." He tapped the cross around his neck. "We'll go tomorrow, then, if you're not too busy. Also," he stood up out of his armchair and gestured for me to follow, walking to a door near the bathroom and opening it. "This is the room I was telling you about."

I stood and walked over to the door, looking inside. The room had a few boxes in it neatly packed into one corner along with a small closet. A bed sized for an ogre sat under the window and took up most of the floor space. Between the bed and the boxes, there was no room for more furniture beyond a bedside table with a lamp and a digital alarm clock on it.

"I use it for the kids when they visit, but they won't be back until next Christmas. Brekur usually sleeps here when he's up." T shrugged a massive shoulder. "It's not a lot of space, I know, but—"

"Before sleeping on the street, I lived in a janitor's closet at St. Mary's," I said, cutting him off. "This is more space than I know what to do with." When I'd first fallen, Father John had let me sleep in the church proper. He'd cleared out a janitor closet and given me a cot, some space for my backpack, and a place for me to hang clothes. The space had been about a third of the room T was offering me. "You're serious? I can stay here?"

T fixed me with a long look, his expression solemn. "I took the measure of you today while you were working. And while we've been talking. I like you, and I think you're honest, hardworking, and trustworthy. Plus, Dust's a great judge of character, so if he says you're all right, I trust him. If you want to stay here, then you can stay. That's all there is to it." He leaned on the wall, looking down at me. "I know what it's like to need help. Plus, we're supposed to take care of people, yeah? Never know when you might be hosting angels."

I smiled. He had no idea how close to the truth he was. "Is that something you believe in?"

"Well, the Bible says it happens. And I trust the Word, so..." He waggled a hand. "I'm no scholar or anything. I leave that to the pastors and priests and whatnot. I just know it says to love people the best you can, yanno? Help those who need helping. Love those who need loving. And sometimes, you flip tables when people get outta line and start doing things they shouldn't."

"Of all the explanations of the Bible's intent, I think I may like yours the most." He was right, too. While the Bible was hardly the only authority on the will of the Father, Tremor had more or less boiled the edicts down into the simplest and most correct explanation I'd ever heard.

T grinned his lopsided grin. "So, you staying?"

"I think the Father guided me to you exactly when I needed you. If I am not in your way, I will stay here, yes."

"Good." T nodded and then yawned, stretching. "I need to crash. I'll wake you up for breakfast, but you can stay up and watch TV or whatever," he said, straightening from where he leaned on the wall and wandering down toward his bedroom. "Goodnight, Cass."

"Goodnight." I looked back at the room — my room — considering the changes in my circumstances. From the church to my friends' homes, from their homes to the street, and from the street to here. It was a massive improvement from sleeping under the bridge, but I felt awful about leaving the people I'd come to know there. Though at least they hadn't seemed to begrudge my change in circumstances. Perhaps there was a way I could help them.

I gathered my backpack and few things from the living room and walked into the space Tremor had said was mine, setting the backpack down under the bedside table and folding my clean clothes atop it. I then closed the door and lay down on the bed.

My phone went off with a text from Eirlas. "You got a minute?"

"Yes."

The phone then rang, and I answered it. "Everything all right?" I asked, concerned that something might have happened. Perhaps demons had attacked or... I didn't know what.

"Yes and no. Father Demoyne came at me and Dust pretty hard today, and I'm... It's not really against what the Bible says that he and I are..." He sounded shaken.

Anger rose in my chest. "No. You loving each other is not against any true law. Remember what I said about the Bible not being the whole story? Beyond that, the Son never mentioned any of that in there, did he."

"Not... that I've ever read. But I don't have the whole thing memorized like you, Cass."

I let out a slow, deep sigh, reminding myself that mortal beings had an incomplete view of the greater whole. That didn't make Father Demoyne's bigotry easier to swallow, but it helped me remember that Eirlas couldn't know and didn't have the tools to fight back. "Despite people's limited understanding and trouble translating and adding things in there that aren't supposed to be, the Bible said nothing at all about homosexuality. The Father made you as you are. And you and Dust loving each other is beautiful, perfect, and holy. Anyone who says otherwise is a fool." I managed to keep my frustration out of everything but the last few words.

"You're... you're sure?" The plaintive, timid, hurting question broke my heart. I wished I were closer so I could hug him until that scared, sad tone went away.

"I am more certain on that than I am on most things in this world. The Father has nothing but love for you and Dust. Don't let Father Demoyne get in your head."

"Yeah… yeah." I could almost see him rubbing a hand over his face. "He cornered me in my office and was lecturing me, and I just… I know he's an ass. I just…"

"You needed to hear the truth from someone who knows."

"Yeah."

I grunted. "Well, that's the truth as I know it, Eirlas. And I wouldn't lie about something so important. Anyone who tells you that your love is wrong or lesser somehow is just wrong."

"Thanks, Cass. I, uh, just… really needed to hear that."

"Of course."

"I'll let you get to bed."

We rang off, and I set my phone on the bedside table. I found myself too upset to sleep immediately, so I pulled out the book I'd borrowed from Jim and read until I dozed off.

# CHAPTER 17

The next morning, I woke to a soft tapping on the door to my room. My room. The thought made me smile, and I sat up, swinging my legs off the bed. "I'm up."

T opened the door a little. "Breakfast in ten. You've got time for a shower if you're quick." He then closed the door again, leaving me my privacy. It felt strange to think of this space as my own, and I wasn't entirely sure how long I'd be here. After having lived on Earth for nearly two years now, I'd slept in so many places for a night or two that only the church really felt like home. And even then, it was more the people in it than the building.

I gathered my clean clothes and toiletries and ambled into the bathroom, where I took a short shower. I'd learned how to do that early on at the shelter. Often people were waiting, so it was just a matter of washing up as quickly as possible so everyone had both hot water and the opportunity to get clean. When I stepped out, I noticed T had put a second towel out for me. That small gesture made me smile again as I dried off and hung the towel back up to dry before dressing. I brushed my teeth and combed my hair, then returned my few toiletries to my room before heading toward the kitchen.

As I got close, I saw T standing at the stove, humming something and bobbing his head as he poured batter into a pan to make the biggest pancakes I had ever seen. Of course, I had been around Dust long enough to know tusked people had huge appetites to go with their size, but nonetheless, it still surprised me. I watched him cook, lingering in the door and unsure what I could do to help. If he needed any.

"Table's all set. You can take a load off. Food's almost done — this is the last one."

"Okay." I moved away from the door and sat down at the table. He'd added a second chair for me, I noticed. How long had he been awake? Pancakes, the second towel, the chair. It showed he'd been up and moving longer than

I had, for certain. I felt awkward just sitting there, waiting for him, but I survived the few minutes between T telling me to sit and him setting a heaping plate of pancakes between us.

"Take what you like. I made enough." He smiled and sank into his chair, plunging his fork into a few pancakes and dragging them onto his plate where he slathered them in "Miss Magpie's Pancake Syrup." It featured a portly, smiling fae woman on the bottle and claimed to add a little magic to one's breakfast. "Also, don't give any to Tiny. He'll get fat."

Tiny had scooted into the room and rested his head on my thigh, staring up at me with such hope that I felt an immense sense of guilt at the idea of denying him. A little pancake surely couldn't hurt. I sneaked him pieces as I ate, trying to disguise it. T either politely ignored my rule breaking or didn't notice. Of course, when Tiny lumbered over to T and repeated the process, T broke his own rules and also fed him bits of pancake while pretending to ignore him entirely. The whole scene was ridiculous enough that I had to fight from laughing and did my best to act as if both of us hadn't just thoroughly broken the edict.

I ate less than T did by a significant margin. The syrup didn't seem to add any magic to my meal that I could tell, though it *did* have a strange, blue-purple sheen to it in the light. Maybe that was the supposed magic. Either way, it tasted vaguely maple-like, and T's pancakes proved to be quite good.

"You comin' in to work today?" T asked around bites of his breakfast.

I nodded. "I had planned to."

"Good. When we get to the shop, we'll get you a schedule that fits what you need. That way, you can live your life and get things done. I'm going to get you a key made so you can get in and out of the building and the apartment."

I already had keys for the church, so that at least was familiar. I nodded and went to speak, but my phone buzzed in my pocket. I didn't recognize the number, which Jim had told me sometimes meant people trying to scam me. I had learned as much after repeated calls telling me my vehicle's extended warranty was out of date. I had panicked the first few times I received messages saying my social security number was under investigation, though.

Jim had calmed me, reminding me I didn't have one, so it wasn't possible. That and the police didn't work like that. "Hello?"

"Cass?" I recognized Axton's voice over the phone.

"Yes, Mister Graves."

"Got your number from Jim. I'm going to be running down a few leads today. If there really are demons going after this thing, I'd kind of like to have you with me in case things go sideways."

"If things go sideways, I advise standing upright. Or..." I frowned. The idea of everything going sideways confused me so much, I craned my head to the side to mimic it in an attempt to understand how that would work.

T just watched and tilted his head some, his expression perplexed. Tiny, who was still lingering in the kitchen, matched the action, obviously not wanting to be left out.

An annoyed noise came over the phone. "Ugh. Angels. Always so literal. In case things get out of control."

I grimaced. Another expression. "Oh, uh, yes. I have work today, but—"

T shook his head, cutting me off. "Remember what I said? Only if you didn't have important things."

"Work, huh?" Axton sounded surprised. "Well, I've got to get things done. You going to be done at five?"

"Yes. I work from nine to five."

Axton hummed something I didn't recognize as though it were a joke. "See you at five, then."

"All right. I will meet you at five." I gave him the address of the shop and we rang off, and I put my phone away. "I will meet Mister Graves at five. He is free then," I repeated to T, who nodded.

"You sure?"

"That was what he said, yes."

"All right. Well, finish your breakfast, and we'll get moving. We've got some stuff to do before work," T said, standing up and gathering his dishes while I finished my food.

Tiny returned his head to my leg, and I frowned down at him. "Are you not ever fed?"

"Oh, he's had breakfast," T answered from the kitchen. "Twice."

"You are gluttonous." I poked the dog in the nose and ignored his hopeful gaze with more ease this time, comforted in the knowledge he had already been very much fed. Dogs, apparently, were bottomless pits into which one threw table scraps and kibble.

After finishing my food, I helped T clean up in the kitchen, and we left the apartment to head to work, or so I thought. Instead, T took me to Walmart and bought me a few sets of jeans and several t-shirts. Given my measurements, we mostly stuck to the men's section, though after a little while, T gave me a sidelong look.

"You sure you're a woman?" he asked. "Not that it matters to me, but you don't..." He trailed off, his brow furrowing. "It doesn't seem like it fits you. The way you carry yourself, the way you talk. That isn't to say you aren't one or aren't feminine enough or anything. You just don't seem like it works."

I shrugged. Father John had once asked me about pronouns and such when we'd first met, but I didn't know much more now than I had then. "It's complicated. I don't know what I am."

"Well, what feels right to you?" he asked, browsing through a rack of plaid flannel shirts.

"Nothing feels right," I admitted with a sigh. "Female was what they called me at the hospital, so I assumed..."

"Nah. You just be what makes sense for you. Lots of species out there don't even have genders. Some of the fae—dryads, I think—mostly reproduce with pollen. There are some kinds of gnomes that come outta rocks. They don't even have parents. Point is, if you don't think you're a woman, you don't have to be one."

I considered his point in silence for a while as I flipped through the clothes. To be honest, my gender was the least of my concerns. Though I was more often mistaken for a man on the street than I was taken for a woman. "I'm not sure I am either a man or a woman," I answered finally. Before I fell, after all, I hadn't possessed reproductive organs at all, so the change was peculiar, to say the least. The idea of being a woman didn't upset me, however. Nor did the idea of being a man.

"Non-binary, then?"

"What does that even mean?" I asked, frowning at the unfamiliar term.

"Means you're neither. Or both. I don't know a lot about it, but like I said, I know there's all kinds of things out there that reproduce different ways, so what do I know." He shrugged.

"I suppose that fits. What is binary?"

T tried to explain it to me but ultimately just pulled out his phone, looked it up, and handed it to me. It turned out to be some sort of computer thing made up of ones and zeroes. How that related to gender, I couldn't imagine, but I accepted the term. T tried to explain, saying that "binary" referred to being one thing or another. Black or white. Not both. The analogy was imperfect, he admitted, but it was the best he knew how to explain it. Being non-binary meant being both or neither. A two in a world of ones and zeroes.

That description matched up to how I felt in so many ways in my life. Not male, not female. Not celestial, not mortal. In this world but not of it. It worked for me.

"If you're non-binary, then, you want me to use different pronouns?"

More questions I couldn't answer. "It's too complicated," I said, trying to stop my head from spinning. "I'm just sticking with what I have. It's too much."

T nodded. "It feels like it sometimes. Seems like you don't know a lot about the world, Cass. I didn't mean to overwhelm you." His expression was apologetic.

T paid for the clothes up front. Two pairs of jeans along with a selection of long-sleeved shirts, a couple flannels, and a small selection of t-shirts. He also threw in two pairs of shoes—heavy work boots and a pair of sneakers. None of it was, by his estimation, expensive, and when I asked him about paying for it, he laughed. He then helped me carry my new clothes out of the store and to his truck.

"No. I came from a very, very different place than this." How else was I going to explain that I came from Heaven, had fallen, and now lived here? With all the kindness he'd shown me, the last thing I wanted to do was jeopardize everything by telling him the truth. Mercifully, he didn't ask for more details.

We drove to his shop listening to the radio after that, though the quiet was companionable. I got the impression he was trying to give me space to sort myself out, which was kind of him.

It dawned on me to perhaps talk to Jim and the others about this whole non-binary thing since I could be candid with them about it. Maybe they could help. That, however, would have to wait until after work and then after my meeting with Axton. There was too much to do, and my identity conundrum would have to wait.

# CHAPTER 18

The day went much like my time at the shop had the day before. T showed me how to perform simple tasks and then kept an eye on me while I did them. He had me clean the place, change oil, answer the phones, and learn how to use the computer system, which was by far the most complex of the jobs. Prior to that, I had never used one for longer than a few minutes. Father John had tried once, but I had gotten lost and frustrated immediately, so he hadn't pressed.

T let me hunt-and-peck my way through typing things when there were no customers. If something time sensitive showed up, he nudged me aside and took over. The software he used sorted everything into neat little boxes where the information went. I didn't know what most of it was (VIN, make, model…), but I could copy words off his intake form into the fields well enough. When lunch rolled around, he ordered us meatball subs from a nearby delivery place and sat with me in the office to eat them.

On one hand, it felt strange to have so much of my time scheduled out like this. On the other, I found the idea of work pleasant. It made me feel like I was making a difference for something. In reality, I was probably more in T's way than I was helpful in those early days. His patience never wavered through all of it, no matter how many times I made mistakes. He just helped me clean them up and told me where I'd gone wrong and to get back to it. Mistakes, he told me, were part of the mortal condition. Everyone made them. The only thing you could do when you screwed up was apologize and learn to do better.

His gentle, paternal guidance felt warm and familiar in ways I had no words for, and I found myself sinking into it like a warm blanket. As dearly as I loved Jim, and as comfortable as I was with him, T had a different air to him. Maybe it was that he'd raised kids. I couldn't tell.

When five rolled around and T and I closed up shop, Axton met me out front in his nondescript black sedan. It was, much like everything in Axton's life seemed to be, an older model vehicle that he took good care of. Well used, but also well cared for. When T saw it, he raised a brow. "Haven't seen one of them in a while," he commented as Axton gestured to me. "Ask him when the last time he changed his oil was."

"I will." I smiled and patted T's arm. "I will call you when I am on my way back to the apartment."

"Home, Cass. When you're on your way *home*."

The word felt foreign, but I nodded. "When I am on my way home."

He grinned at me and headed around back toward his truck while I met up with Axton, who opened the passenger-side door for me to get into the car.

When I'd settled myself, he looked at the garage. "You learn anything since we talked yesterday?" he asked.

"Not about our goal, no. Though I did learn how to change oil. T wants me to ask when the last time you had your car's oil changed was."

Axton laughed. I must have caught him off guard. "You know. A while ago." Shaking his head, he sobered. "Listen, I know someone who might be able to help us. Emphasis on *might*. I haven't talked to her in a while, but it's the only lead I've got."

"All right. And you want me to go with you for what reason?"

His lip curled a little in something between a sneer and a snarl. There was the Axton I'd come to expect. "Because this particular friend of mine has a soft spot for sad charity cases and, well..." He gestured to all of me.

I grunted in reply, feeling like that was unnecessarily rude. I still couldn't figure him out. While he was nice enough to everyone else, I had the distinct and deep-seated feeling he despised me for reasons I didn't understand. It stung, but I had experienced such rejection before from people who decided they hated me on principle. Father John had taken care to teach me that such things weren't my fault. I couldn't, after all, control others' feelings.

It was Jim who had told me that reactions like that usually had nothing to do with the person they were being taken out on. Whatever had made Axton dislike me so intensely must have fallen into that category since, no matter how many times I replayed our interactions in my head, I couldn't understand what I'd done to elicit such hostility.

Axton put the car in gear and pulled out into the lane, navigating through the narrow, winding streets.

Unlike many other large cities which are laid out in a grid pattern, Boston more closely resembles a dropped plate of spaghetti with street names on it. Given that it grew out of a small colony, and most of the roads were created by people on horseback avoiding obstacles, it is a disaster to navigate. It seems most often to be a mess of one-way streets going every direction but the one you are trying to go, and God help you if there is construction.

There is always construction.

"Where, exactly, are we going?" I asked as we headed toward the heart of the city.

Axton shot me a look. "She runs a charity. Immigrants and such arriving in the city can go to her to get help."

"She sounds like a very kind woman," I said, trying to keep my tone pleasant. "But why would she know where to find a magical artifact in the city?" I had learned from watching Jim interact with people that sometimes, the best thing you could do was not rise to the bait.

"Because that woman knows *everything*." He didn't explain further.

When we arrived at the office, it turned out to be in a three-story brick building with the office in question on the third floor. A tarnished bronze plaque near the door read "Refugee Immigration Services," and inside the office was yet another waiting room. I was growing all too familiar with those of late. This one was neat, smelled like some kind of incense, and had broad, south-facing windows that caught the light, creating a sort of spiritual warmth in addition to the obvious heat from the sunlight.

Axton didn't sit down to wait. Instead, he opened a door and walked into a hallway with several offices branching off it until he reached the last door on the left. He stopped and tapped on the door with his knuckles. "Ruth?"

"Come in," a sweet, older woman's voice replied.

Despite his gruff manner with me, he fixed his hair in the hallway and straightened his shoulders some before opening the door, like he cared what Ruth thought of his appearance. I didn't comment on his fussing since it seemed like a quick way getting even further on his bad side.

When he opened the door, it revealed an office I could only describe as "cozy." Books were stuffed onto every surface and lined the walls, and several overstuffed chairs took up much of the floor space near the desk. The desk itself was humble enough but seemed to be a repository for yet more books and papers. A tall plant of some kind stood in a corner near the window, drinking in the sunlight.

The woman herself was soft. Her white hair was swept back from her face in a bun, and her eyes were surrounded by the sort of wrinkles one gets when they smile a lot throughout a lifetime. There were lines of sorrow, too, but right now, all I really noticed was the joy because when she smiled, it was the kindest expression I had ever seen.

"Axton," she said. "It's good to see you."

"You too, Ruth," he said, returning the smile in a way I hadn't seen before. He flopped down into one of the chairs, not introducing me.

I lingered near the door, not sure if I was supposed to come in or not until Ruth gestured to me. "Come in, come in. Close the door. No use hanging about in the hallway."

Her gentle chiding encouraged me, and I did as she instructed, sitting in the unoccupied seat in front of her desk.

"You didn't introduce me to your friend," Ruth said with a note of gentle reproach.

"Not a friend. A client. Cass, this is Ruth. Ruth, this is Cass." Axton gestured between us with a careless wave. "We're looking for something, and you're the only person I can think of who might know where to find it."

She steepled her fingers, joints swollen with arthritis. I suspected she was human, given the lack of overt signs of anything else, but I could only guess. "I see. So this isn't a social visit, then."

"No, I'm afraid not." Axton shook his head. "We heard a rumor that something big is in the city. An item of significant power and of serious importance to the church. Have you heard of anything coming through that would fit that description?"

"Whatever do you want something like that for? Last I knew, you were avoiding the church. Not that I blame you, given..." She trailed off and glanced at me as if stopping herself from saying something I shouldn't hear. "Well. Not that I blame you."

Axton sighed like a balloon someone was letting the air out of. I could practically see him deflate. "I am. I was. I don't want to be involved in this, but if Cass is right," he jerked a thumb at me, "then all of this could get really bad for a lot of people who don't deserve it. And I can't just walk away from that."

"Of course you can't." Ruth nodded once, her expression knowing. "Most of the major artifacts in the area are well-guarded. There's nothing new that I know of." She turned to me finally, fixing me with an intent expression. "So what is it you're after and why?"

Something about her eyes gave me pause. They looked normal enough, but it felt like she could see something about me that I wasn't sure I wanted anyone to know. I glanced at Axton. "Should…"

"She knows."

I took a slow, deep breath. "I am a fallen. Cassiel. I was a gate guardian. I recently learned that one of the nails of the cross is here in the city. There are demons after it, and I am hoping to get to it before they do."

Ruth listened as I spoke, her expression calm. As if the information neither surprised nor dismayed her. After a moment, her lips turned up, eyes twinkling. "Oh, is that all?"

# CHAPTER 19

I looked at Axton and then back at Ruth. "Is that all?" I asked, incredulous.

Ruth chuckled. "I was mostly joking," she said. "If what you're saying is true, then obviously things are quite serious." She sat back in her chair, lacing her fingers together on her desk and considering. "If there is a nail from the cross in the city, it's not here on an official visit. At least not that I've been made aware of. Which means it's likely been here longer than I have which, as you know, Axton, is quite some time." She pulled a legal pad closer to herself, jotting down notes in spidery handwriting that I doubted I could have read if I'd been looking at it straight, let alone upside down.

Axton sat forward in his chair. "There are the usual vaults where that kind of thing might be kept. The protected places. But I'm not aware of any of *those* in the city."

"Neither am I." Ruth shook her head and frowned at her notes for a very long time, as though the pen and ink would yield their secrets and produce answers.

I waited as patiently as I could while she mulled over the problem, despite the desire to reach across the table and shake her until the answer came out. It wouldn't, I knew, do any good, but the instinct remained. Instead, I leaned back in the chair and let my knee start bouncing some as I waited for her to give us some sort of insight. The activity helped get some of the extra energy out, though it didn't provide any flashes of brilliance, much to my dismay.

Axton gave me a look but didn't say anything, and I stopped.

"They're not doing anybody any harm by being anxious, Axton," Ruth said without looking up, her tone admonishing but not unkind. "Let them fidget."

"She," Axton corrected. This time when he looked at me, it was for confirmation. "Right?" For all he could be an ass at times, the correction and attempt at respect made me smile at him.

I nodded. "She."

"Let *her* fidget, then." Ruth sat back, gliding over the change without lifting her eyes from her notepad. "As I'm sure you've already considered, I'd start with the historical churches and cemeteries. That's the most logical place to hide such a thing if you're trying to keep it out of demonic hands."

Axton sighed heavily and rubbed his forehead. "This city's full of old churches and graveyards, which is part of the problem. Assuming it's even in one. For all we know, it could literally just be a nail in a building somewhere, holding up part of an old wall. If I had any idea when it came into the city — or even country — or who brought it, we'd have a starting place, but as it is..." He trailed off. "Which is why I'm here. If I was going to hunt through every old church yard and cemetery in the city, I'd be out there now."

"I can put my ear to the ground for you and see what's out there. If anything. But I don't know anything off the top of my head. Relics like *that* don't usually just pop up uninvited. The Vatican — "

"I know, I know." Axton grunted and waved a hand. "The Vatican has most of 'em under lock and key."

"Why do the Catholics have so many?" I asked, looking between them. I knew what the Vatican was, more or less, since Father John had explained it. I found the whole concept of the Pope uncomfortable, but I'd kept my mouth shut on that score. Of course, there were a great deal of things to do with the workings of the church that I disliked. I had learned over time to recognize that those were mortal additions. They needed structure, so they did what made sense to them.

"Have you ever heard of the Crusades?" Ruth asked.

I shook my head.

"A long time ago, the Catholic church was convinced it was the only truth in the world. It waged war across the Middle East trying to claim land between Europe and Jerusalem. Part of that group was a sect called the Knights Templar. They worked directly for the church and were rumored to be hunting for the Holy Grail."

"The Holy Grail?" I raised a brow.

"The supposed cup that caught the blood of Jesus when he died," Axton answered.

I made a revolted noise, not only for the hubris of the world, but also the notion of collecting someone's blood like that. What would be the point? "That seems like a very strange thing to do, let alone keep."

Ruth nodded. "Indeed. While they were out there killing people in the name of God — whose commandments include not murdering people — they scooped up as many artifacts of power as they could, storing them away. Then, as England continued to colonize the world, and the Vatican grew in power, they used that reach to continue the process. As a result, they have a large percentage — if not most — of those items locked away in vaults hidden around the world."

Axton looked away through the conversation, as if trying to avoid it. I didn't understand why, but his discomfort was palpable, even to me. His shoulders had tensed, and he was studying Ruth's bookshelf far more intensely than necessary, like he could set fire to them with the power of his mind. I wanted to ask him what was wrong but thought better of it. After all, we weren't friends, and I doubted he would want to discuss it with me of all people.

"The Vatican, of course," Ruth continued, "denies all of this. They claim they have no such things, and that the relics of monks and priests and such are merely historically significant. Worshiping the saints is risky business when it comes to being monotheistic anyway." She shrugged. "Not that it makes more sense to keep the finger bone of someone who performed magic a few hundred years ago any more than it does to keep blood from the Son. Either way, the Vatican has most of these items we know about hidden away where the rest of the world either doesn't know they exist or can't reach them.

"While I'm not excited at the idea of them having claimed so much power over the years, I can say that it does mean that fewer of those relics are out in the world, which does help cut down on the chaos. And some of them are extremely dangerous in the wrong hands, so in some ways, it's just as well they're kept out of the way," Ruth said, her expression contemplative. "Even if I don't always trust the hands they're in, either."

I sighed. "There is so much killing and... and stupidity in the name of the Father." The idea hurt because I knew, down in the bones of me, that it wasn't what He wanted. In fact, His hope was for quite the opposite.

"What's worse is they're all arguing about fragments of knowledge none of them understand."

Resting her hands on the legal pad, Ruth nodded, her expression solemn. "If there is one thing I have learned in my many years, it is that none of us really know the mind of God. But if I have to err on the side of something, it's going to be on the side of kindness, justice, and love."

I smiled despite myself. "You remind me of someone else I know," I said, thinking back to T who had said almost the same thing.

"Then your friend is very wise." She smiled and looked in Axton's direction. "I wish I could do more, but other than making some calls, I'm not sure if I can give you the answers you're looking for. If I were you, I would pray for guidance."

Axton grunted and made a face like he'd bitten into something bitter. "I'll leave that to you."

"Perhaps my prayers will be enough for all of us, then. But more certainly can't hurt."

"I'll pray," I volunteered. It wasn't like I hadn't been already. "Thank you for your desire to help." I stood, getting the feeling we had imposed on her long enough, and she didn't have the information we needed.

Axton rose, offering Ruth his hand. Instead of shaking it, he just held it and squeezed a little, the contact warm and careful. "I'll be in touch."

Ruth shook his hand and then turned to me, offering me her hand, palm up.

I took it gently. "Thank you." She surprised me with a firm handshake that belied her hands' arthritic appearance. Along with that came the faint thrill of something familiar, though I couldn't put my finger on it because it happened so quickly, I almost thought I imagined it.

"You're welcome, Cass. I'm sorry I couldn't do more to help. You stay safe out there, hm?"

"I'll do my best."

Axton and I left Ruth's office and walked back down to his car in silence. Ruth had put me at ease somehow, though I couldn't discern why. Axton, on the other hand, had his hands thrust so deep in his pockets, I was concerned he'd tear through them. I could almost imagine him as a hive of wasps, angry and buzzing. I decided not to try my luck with talking to him and just got into the car with him once we reached it.

When we pulled away from the curb, Axton didn't volunteer where we were headed, so I just looked out the window and watched the streets go by. If this was really to be such a trial, and there was no way of knowing even where to start, I despaired finding this before the demons I was trying to subvert did. Realistically, it was a needle in a haystack, and I knew it. And without the ability to get more information out of Codiel, the only resource I had was a demon who wanted to play "Hot and Cold" with me.

This was going great.

# CHAPTER 20

A xton and I spent the next several hours driving around the city. We visited cemeteries and old churches and yet more cemeteries. Most of the historical cemeteries we couldn't just walk into—particularly this time of night. Chain fences surrounded them to keep interlopers out and protect the historical graves from modern vandals. Instead, we walked around them, and Axton had me reach out for anything that might be the nail.

With it being winter, the sun had set early and plunged us into darkness. That, and a storm had rolled in, causing the shadows to rise even earlier. Heavy, white snowflakes fell, driven by the wind hard enough that they ran horizontal to the car, and our progress through the city had become a crawl as Axton fought both weather and traffic. Plows rumbled through the gathering slush, dumping salt on the road and carving throughfares on the arterial roads, but the side roads were getting slick.

"Maybe we should wrap this up for the night?" I suggested, breaking the silence between us. Other than giving me basic instructions for what we were doing at the various sites we visited, he hadn't said a word to me during the drive. By then, though, I was tired, hungry, and my back felt like someone was taking a hammer to it. Sitting against the seat as I was had irritated the deep gouge between my shoulders, and every movement felt like I was grinding broken glass into the wound.

"No." His tone gave no room for argument.

I argued anyway. "I don't know that we have made any significant headway, and we're going to make less as the weather gets worse. Also, I am very hungry. I would like to return home so I can eat and—"

"There are *demons* out there trying to get their nasty hands on an item of that kind of power, and you're worried about missing *dinner*?" He glared at me, jaw clenched, eyes blazing. "What the hell kind of angel are you?"

His comment stung, and I looked away, clenching my jaw shut. Instead of snapping back at him, I looked out the window, my knee bouncing a little again until I forced it to stop, not wanting to annoy Axton further.

Axton sighed and rubbed his face with both hands as we paused at a stoplight. "I'm sorry," he said, his tone softer. "I'll stop somewhere and get us food." We were both exhausted, and the strain of having no information was fraying our nerves to dust. I understood; I wasn't my best at that moment, either.

"I know it's none of my business, and you don't like me, but Jim says it helps to express what you're feeling. I can tell this situation is upsetting you about more than just the demons."

He was quiet for so long, I thought he must be ignoring me before he finally spoke up. "I am very, very old, and I worked for the church for a long time. We didn't part on good terms, and all of this is just dragging that back up again." Axton stared out the windshield, hands clenched around the steering wheel, not looking at me. "I've dealt with a lot of angels over the years, and most of 'em were jerks." The way he chose his words reminded me a bit of Ether and her hatred for religion, and it clicked. He had been hurt.

"I am trying very hard not to be one."

"I know. My problems with all of this aren't your fault." He sighed again, his shoulders slouching. "Me taking this out on you isn't fair, and I know it. But you have to understand how complicated all of this is for me." As apologies went, it was weak, but it felt genuine.

"How can I understand if you don't tell me?" I asked. "Before this moment, you have told me nothing about your involvement in this. I know you don't like me, and I have been trying not to take that personally, but I cannot understand how difficult something is for a person if they do not tell me."

I tried to keep the sharp edges out of my voice and let go of the hurt and anger he'd been inspiring in me since we met. He wasn't obligated to tell me his life's story — or anything at all not pertaining to the case — but I felt like he owed me this much. Maybe it was how tired I was or how much I was hurting, but I didn't feel charitable enough to just let him continue with it.

His jaw clenched again, but Axton nodded instead of taking my head off. "You know what a gar is?" he asked, risking a quick glance in my direction before turning his attention back to the road.

I shook my head.

"Long ago—back in Medieval days—there was a dragon called the Gargouille. I don't know everything about him, but he was rampaging around Northern France sometime in the 600s. A bishop, seeking to help the people but also to display the power of faith, hunted down and subdued the beast. He forced the dragon to follow him back to town and burned him at his church."

Dragons. By now, they're all extinct so far as most anybody knows. They certainly haven't been prominent since the Medieval period when most of the western ones were hunted out. In the east, they all just vanished. There are rumors they went into hiding in obscurity to avoid the fate that befell the dragons in the west. The church, in particular, hated them and did their best to exterminate the whole species, claiming they were servants of the devil.

"Behind closed doors, using holy magics and the ashen remains of the Gargouille, they crafted beings of living stone to serve the church's needs."

"Living stone?" I asked, the concept confusing me. Stone, after all, was definitely not alive. At least that I had ever seen.

Axton grinned. "You've never seen my true form. The Gar," he explained, "are guardians, created to serve and protect the church and their holdings. They were made to carry out the will of the church and its hierarchy. Beholden to them. Bound to duty."

I frowned. "That sounds like slavery."

He glanced at me. "You think? But I suspect they figured, if God created his angels to serve him, why couldn't they create servants of their own? The hubris of man." He grunted.

"Anyway, the Gar were given compulsions and abilities which make us powerful protectors. We even have the ability to be conduits to channel holy energy and pure Grace to work directly with angels to guard places, items, or beings of great power. Which is what you felt back in my office."

He sighed. "I managed to get away from that life long ago. Took my freedom and ran with it. Mostly managed to avoid anything to do with holy relics, the

Catholics, and pretty much all of that for centuries. And here you are, upsetting my apple cart. I can't even turn down this job because if I do, a lot of innocent people will likely get hurt, and that's the kind of thing I'm in business to try and prevent."

I nodded, considering everything he'd said, even if some of the implications were lost on me at the time because I had no real understanding of dragons or the true scope of the church's power.

Let me be clear here, though. I don't hate the Catholics or the Vatican. They are, like everyone else, people. There are good and bad. Altruistic and selfish. Faithful and those who would twist the religion to their own ends for power. Some are foolish, some are intelligent. This is true even of clergy. Father John, for example, was one of the gentlest, most loving souls I could imagine. Father Demoyne, on the other hand, is an ass.

All that said, it's indisputable, historical fact that atrocities have been committed in the name of the Father by people claiming to serve His will.

They aren't.

"I'm sorry that happened to you, Axton." I let my voice soften as the anger drained out of me. "I can't atone for it since I had no hand in it. I don't understand how any angel could, but I don't blame you for your dislike of me or what I must represent to you. Once we're finished here, I will not ask for your help again." What else could I say? After all, my kindred and those theoretically serving them had done him grievous injury. His bitterness about this case became clear to me, and I realized he was making a significant personal sacrifice to get this done.

A deep, heavy sigh left him, and Axton shook his head, taking a corner slowly to avoid spinning out in the worsening slush on the streets. "It's not your fault." He pulled up to the curb outside yet another church. I'd started to lose count of them by then.

I got out, prepared to repeat the same vague search we'd done on all the other buildings. Axton went one way around it, and I went the other, reaching out to try and feel for any source of significant Grace. However, instead of Grace, I felt Blight. It wasn't far from me off in the opposite direction of the church, and I turned my head to look toward it, holy fire igniting around my fists.

"So paranoid, angel," Asakku said, stepping out of the shadows of an alleyway and coming alongside me. He was wearing a different suit than he had been earlier. This time, his tie was a sunfire orange color, and his black suit had pinstripes of the same shade running through them. His shirt—of which I could barely see the collar, a slight "v" behind the tie, and the cuffs of his sleeves flashing from under his coat sleeves—was a dark burgundy.

I grunted and released the power I'd gathered, letting the flames go out. "This surprises you?"

"Not at all. But it *is* amusing. I figured, since you're out sniffing, I'd let you know that you are so very, very cold right now." He grinned. "And I don't just mean in temperature."

"This is ridiculous," I said, planting my feet and crossing my arms, glaring at him. "After what, ten places, you show up *now*?"

His shoulders rose and fell in a careless shrug. "Do you believe yourself to be the only pressing matter on my plate? I only came to inform you, you have been cold. No closer than before."

"I have an entire *city* to search through, demon. If this is such a pressing thing, and you are in such a hurry, perhaps you could actually help rather than pop out of shadows to jab at me." I glowered at him, which only seemed to deepen his amusement.

"Feisty. I like it." His smile didn't falter even as I growled. "Fine, then. A hint since you're obviously making no headway. Are you ready?"

My hands itched to grab him by the neck, but instead, I took a slow, deep breath and released it in a plume of steam. "Fine."

Asakku moved close to me again, his lips almost brushing my ear, heat radiating from him at the proximity and seeping into my cold skin. It would have felt wonderful if not for the source. "One if by land; two if by sea." He then straightened while I rubbed my ear, trying to make the strange tickling sensation he'd inspired fade.

"How in the world is that useful for anything? It's in the water?"

"You have your hint. Now off you go."

"Somehow, I feel more confused than I did before you gave me a hint."

"Did you forget?"

I frowned. "Forget what?"

"I *am* a demon." He winked with that Cheshire smile and vanished just as Axton rounded the corner of the church and approached me, lifting his hands in a gesture suggesting he wanted to know what the hell had held me up.

# CHAPTER 21

I walked up to Axton, still shaking off my annoyance with Asakku. "Does 'one if by land; two if by sea' mean anything to you?"

His expression changed from irritation to confusion. "Uh, yeah. Paul Revere's ride. It's a whole..." When he trailed off, scowling and staring at nothing, I waited. "Old North Church," he said finally. "It's where that whole lanterns thing happened. There've been protests there lately; it's been all over the news. They had some kind of issue with their foundation, and a bunch of water got into the basement. There's a crypt down there; they've been talking about needing to move some of the remains to repair the damage." As he spoke, I could see gears turning. "Shit. That makes sense. Where'd you get that?"

"You remember that demon I mentioned that tipped me off to this whole thing?"

Axton raised a brow. "Uh-huh."

"Him."

"And you're *just now* bringing it up?"

"No, I—"

"Come on." Axton brushed past me toward the car, leaving me to follow him. He climbed into his vehicle and gestured for me to hurry up.

I scuttled to the car, taking care not to slip in the several inches of snow that had accumulated on the pavement by then. When I got in, Axton had the heat on, and he was staring out the windshield. "We aren't going to be able to get in there tonight. They've stopped doing tours because of the protests. Tomorrow, I'll give them a call and see if I can't get us in. With the issues in the crypt, we probably won't be allowed down there, but maybe I can arrange... something." He pulled out into the road. "Either way, I'll pick you up tomorrow morning, and we'll head there."

"So we are done for the night?" I asked, grateful to be going home.

"Yeah. If that information is correct, then we've got a good starting point. Old North was on the list of locations I had, too. It's the oldest church in the city. At this point, though, it's half church and half tourist destination, so I wasn't sure there'd be enough juice there to hold an artifact like that. Too many people coming and going for non-sacred reasons. It's still operating as a church every Sunday, so it's still a house of worship, but it's not quite the same as some of the other places."

"Why would people go to a church if not to worship?" I asked, confounded by the notion.

"It's an important piece of the history of the country," Axton explained. "Old North Church played a big role in the American Revolutionary War, and it's, well, old. At least by American standards. Most of the buildings in this country aren't more than maybe three hundred years old. Unlike Europe, where there are places built in the Roman period that are still inhabited." He shrugged. "The First Nations people didn't do much for permanent structures that weren't destroyed by the colonists. And those that are still around are out west in the desert mostly."

The context helped some, and I nodded. Though the notion of three hundred years being old amused me a little, and I chuckled.

"Yeah, I know," Axton said. "But most of these folks won't live to see much older than a hundred, so three hundred's a long time."

"Who were the First Nations people?" I asked.

"The people who lived on this continent before the Europeans showed up. They go by a lot of names, but I'm told First Nations is the one they use these days. Settlers called 'em Indians."

"...How in the world did they make that mistake?"

Axton shrugged. "Don't ask me. I was asleep at the time."

"Asleep? That is a very long time to be asleep."

An expression of pain crossed his face. "Yeah, well. I was."

At this point, I knew better than to ask, so I didn't. Instead, I focused on the history lesson. "If Old North Church is so," I smirked, "old, then I suppose the nail could've been brought there. You said there is a crypt?"

He nodded, appearing relieved at the change of topic back to the work. "Yeah. I don't know who all is buried down there, but I assume it's mostly priests or important people from the time. Maybe one of them could've smuggled it out of Europe."

"Why?" I frowned, not understanding the implications.

"Things were a mess back then. The Catholics and Protestants were at each other's throats, and a lot of people were leaving the British Isles because of it. Maybe one of them stole it. Or maybe it came down through their family. I don't know. But there are a lot of reasons why they might've brought it here. Hell, they might've been trying to hide it from the Vatican. If it came over here early enough that it's in the crypt of Old North, there weren't a lot of Europeans here at the time, and the Catholics never did get a foothold in the Americas like they did in Europe."

I didn't understand all of that and resolved to learn more about history when I had the time. What little I did understand wasn't any help here, however, so I just nodded along. "All right."

Axton glanced at me. "You don't understand most of that, do you." It wasn't a question.

I blushed.

"All right. Simplest explanation: the Christians were arguing over who was right, and someone wanted to keep the nail away from the Catholic church's greedy little mitts."

"Not so little," I commented. I'd gleaned that much, at least.

"Not so little," Axton agreed. He then took me to get food, as he'd promised. Whatever else he might be, Axton struck me as a man of his word. He talked a little as we drove, maybe making an effort to be kinder to me. I knew an olive branch when I saw one, and I accepted it.

We pulled up to the apartment building that was now my home, and I called T, letting him know I was back. He agreed to let me in. Once I got off the phone, I looked over at Axton, frowning. "Thank you. For explaining this to me. And for taking this job despite everything."

He turned his gaze toward me, expression weary and conflicted. "Yeah. Well, you're not the worst angel I've dealt with, so you have that going for you. Just do me a favor: stay on this side of things, all right? I've seen how easily fallen can be tempted into making bad choices that land them on the dark side. Don't make me regret working with you." He nodded once and then gestured toward the apartment building. "Go on and get some sleep. I'll see you tomorrow morning."

"All right." I nodded and climbed out of the car. His warning hung heavy on me, and I sighed. He wasn't wrong. I couldn't rebut the truth, but that didn't make it any easier to sit with.

Axton pulled away from the curb, and I walked up to the front door of the building. T came down the stairs a moment later and opened it for me.

"Here," he said, handing me a small keyring with two keys on it. "This one's the front door." He pointed to one of them. "This one's the apartment key." They looked more or less the same, but the letter "A" had been scratched into the apartment key. "This way, you can come and go how you need to."

The simple gesture gave me pause. Whether it was exhaustion of the day, frustration from dealing with Asakku and Axton, or overall emotional strain, my throat closed, and I nodded, sniffling once. "Okay."

T looked at me for a second and then drew me into a hug, wrapping his massive arms around me and holding me close. He smelled like engine oil, scotch, and tobacco smoke. His tank top didn't fully cover his chest, and wiry hair spilled out of the top of it, rough against my cheek where he held me.

I clung to him and cried. I cried out of relief of having a home. I cried out of frustration regarding this whole nail situation. I cried because there were people who needed homes and didn't have them while I got a warm bed. I cried because the church had hurt Axton and so many others. I cried because Father John was dead. All of it just poured out of me and soaked into T's shirt.

One of his broad hands moved to the back of my head, and he stroked my hair, his large fingers cradling me close to him. T didn't say a word or ask what was wrong. He didn't try to solve anything. Instead, he just hugged me while the emotions washed over me and let me cry.

When I'd exhausted myself, T gently led me upstairs and into the apartment where he sat me down on the couch. Tiny jumped up beside me and lay his huge head in my lap, and T draped a blanket over my shoulders. He then went into the kitchen while I patted the dog with numb, trembling fingers.

It all felt like so much. I had no idea if I was going to be able to even find the nail, let alone foil the plot to get it.

Or figure out what in the hell Asakku wanted with it before he could snatch it. I didn't know if I could help Dust and Eirlas with Father Demoyne's ill-guided idiocy toward their relationship. Nothing in this world made sense, and all of it seemed like jagged edges and razor blades.

Until T reached a mug over my shoulder. "Here."

I took it from him, and the warmth filled my hands. The scent of hot cocoa wafted up with the steam.

"Careful. It's still hot." T sunk into the chair he'd occupied the night before. "If you wanna talk about it, I'm here to listen. If you don't, I'll shut up and watch television. Or if you wanna talk about anything but what's wrong, I'll... uh," he scratched his jaw, "I'll come up with something."

I smiled a little. While Jim seemed better at convincing me to talk about the things I didn't want to discuss, T just left the door open. "Thank you," I said, my voice shaking some. "It's... it's just been a long day." I didn't know how to explain any of it to him. Not really. "I'm working with Axton to try and find something that could get a lot of people hurt if it ends up in the wrong hands. We're having trouble finding it, and I'm worried that time is running out."

T nodded, his large, dark eyes focused on me. He didn't say anything in response, though, and the silence stretched between us until I felt obligated to fill it with something. Anything.

"You're a man of faith, right?"

"I sure try to be."

"And... you said you take that quote about hosting angels to heart, right?"

"Mm-hmm."

"What if I told you it was true?"

# CHAPTER 22

T leaned back in his chair. "Well, the Bible's supposed to be true, ain't it?"

"I mean literally."

"Okay." He gave me a long, considering look. "You saying you're an angel?"

My gaze dropped to where Tiny lay with his head on my leg, which was making the whole thing start to go a little numb under his considerable weight. I couldn't bring myself to move him, though. He just looked so comfortable. "If I told you I was, would you think I'm crazy?"

T rubbed his jaw again, scratching the stubble there as he thought. He didn't say anything for a long while before he spoke again. "Well, I've only known you a couple days, but I like to think I'm a good judge of character. I don't think you're delusional or anything. But I'm not a shrink." T looked at me again, and I could feel the weight of his gaze on me while I continued to pat Tiny. "But if you are an angel, what're you doing down here, working in my auto shop and sleeping in my guest bedroom?"

It was a fair question, but it was one I didn't want to answer. I had, however, brought the whole thing up and felt like I owed him an explanation. "I... I am fallen."

"Fallen? Cass, the only fallen angels I've ever heard of are like Lucifer and things like that. You're no devil." He snorted at the idea.

"Angels can fall without becoming demons. I made a mistake—a bad one—and was cast out. I've lived in Boston a few weeks shy of two years now." Gently removing Tiny's head from my leg, I stood up. The big dog sulked when I stopped patting him, his tail thundering against the couch cushions. He rolled onto his back with a pleading expression, and I paused long enough to rub his belly as I'd learned he enjoyed.

T watched me, and I took a breath and summoned my wings.

While there are a number of winged humanoid species in the world, seraphim are the only ones I know of with six. Some other angels have four, and then there are the cherubim who have many, but most of the earthbound creatures only ever have two.

T must have known this because when I displayed them, he stared, then slid out of the chair and dropped to his knees, his big hand fumbling for the cross he wore. "Cass," he said, his tone breathless and expression confused. "Cass, is that… really true?" His eyes were wide and childlike, and tears threatened.

Jim had looked away. Dust and Eirlas had nearly fallen over themselves in startled terror. Axton had just stared. T? T wept.

Unsure what to do with myself, I took a few steps toward him and rested my hand on his shoulder. I called a small amount of my Grace to my fingertips and reached down into him with it. He shuddered, but it wasn't pain or fear. It was a huge, gut-wrenching sob. T's hand moved, and he touched my leg, gripping into my jeans, which were still wet from stomping around the city.

"It's okay," I said, feeling a bit awkward about his response. "I'm still just me."

He lifted his head and shook it, smiling through the tears. "It's not that. It's just…" He trailed off as though searching for words. "I believed, like I said I did. But this? It's proof. You are proof. I know my wife is really and truly at peace with the Lord. I know I'll see her again. You have no idea what that means to me."

I knew logically T must have had a wife—he had kids—but he hadn't said anything about her. Though he wore a wedding band. I put the pieces together and realized she must have died. He was a widower.

Much as he had for me, I let him cry. "There are many things I am uncertain of in this world, T," I said softly, "but I am absolutely positive that is the case. You will see her again, and she is at peace with the Father."

He sobbed again, still clinging to my pants and burying his face in my thigh near my knee. Despite the emotional exhaustion and my own worries, warmth filled me. His faith, his sincerity, his love. Maybe the world wasn't so terrible after all. Maybe my despair and my misery weren't all that was in it. If this kind of love existed in the world, then maybe it was still worth fighting for.

After T recovered from the shock and calmed down, I dismissed my wings and returned to sit on the couch and picked up my still-warm cocoa. T wiped his face now and then, clearing his throat a little awkwardly. "So, this thing you're looking for. It's related to you being an angel, isn't it."

I nodded. "Yes. I am trying to find a holy relic before a demon can get to it."

"And that's what you hired Graves for. Was that his name?"

"Yes."

"Does he know?"

I nodded.

"Look, this whole… angels and demons thing is way bigger than I am. But if there's anything I can do to help, I'm willing, all right? I don't know how much Dust told you, but he and I served together in the military. We saw some shit. Uh. Stuff." He flushed and rubbed the back of his head awkwardly. "Probably shouldn't swear around the servant of God."

I shrugged. "I am not bothered by the fact that you 'saw some shit.' But I don't understand what that has to do with fighting. Shit is feces, isn't it?"

T laughed and picked himself up off the floor, returning to his chair. "It's an expression. Means we fought together. Saw some bad things. Dealt with 'em. You know, knowin' you're an angel makes a lot of this make more sense. I was trying to figure out how you'd gone through life not understanding, well, *life* before."

A blush crept up my neck, and I sighed, sitting back on the couch and pulling Tiny into my lap again. He groaned in exuberant pleasure as I resumed my patting. "I'm still trying to understand everything. I haven't really had much of an opportunity to learn."

"Well, you know what? That's something I *can* help you with. Wife and I homeschooled the kids for years, so I can teach you some stuff. It won't be a college education, but… You know, I could ask Torook. He's an actual college professor. Might have some ideas."

I smiled some and had more of the cocoa, feeling warmer and more steady again. Between T's gentle concern, his faith, and his tireless willingness to help, the hard knot of emotion in my chest loosened. "You are very kind."

"I have a literal angel in my apartment. What else am I supposed to do?" He held his hands up.

"In Sodom, the people rallied around outside and were furious that Lot didn't send the angels out to be raped by the masses."

"Yeah, well, this is Boston, not Sodom."

"You make a fair point." The cocoa had warmed me through and relaxed me enough that I felt like I could speak on everything I'd been carrying. "This task I am on. It's dangerous, and I am worried I won't succeed. I've felt like I'm drowning since I discovered all of this."

"This the first time you've dealt with anything like it?"

"No. Last year, I dealt with a demon who was producing drugs. Ripper, specifically. I fought him and smote him. He killed my friend."

T studied me in silence for a while. "I know what it's like to have friends die and not be able to help it. So does Dust. And that buddy of his he told me you're friendly with. What's his name. Uh. Hammerson."

I nodded. "It's horrible."

"You know, Hammerson runs this group at the church for veterans. People who've fought in wars and lost folks fighting. While what you're going through isn't the same, exactly, you're still a soldier fighting a war. Maybe going there would help?"

"Jim's mentioned it a few times. I don't know. I'm not really a soldier the same as you are. I guarded a gate and fought demons. It was different than what you have all been through."

"War's war, Cass. Whether you're fighting demons or enemy soldiers. PTSD is still a reality for us. So's loss. Survivor's guilt. All that bad shit. Stuff. Ah, hell." He groaned, burying his head in his hands.

His attempts to not cuss and annoyance at himself amused me. "You can swear, T. It's not really a sin." I chuckled and shook my head. The things mortal creatures got themselves in knots over.

"It isn't?"

I shook my head. "No. Your intent here isn't to harm me. If you were cussing me out or calling me names or trying to be cruel to me, then it would be a sin. It's not about the words you use; it's about the intent behind them."

"Oh, well, okay. I'm definitely not trying to insult you." He held up his hands again, eyes a little wide as he shook his head.

"I know." I yawned. "I'll consider going to the group. But tomorrow, I am going with Axton to Old North Church to try and find the relic."

"They meet on Tuesdays and Thursdays anyway. Tomorrow's Wednesday." T stood up and took my now-empty cocoa mug from me. "You look like you're about to fall asleep on the couch."

"I feel like I'm about to fall asleep on the couch."

"Hey, uh…" He shifted awkwardly in his chair, not sure how to ask the question clearly hanging in his mind. "Your full name's really Cass?"

I smiled a little. "Cassiel."

"Cassiel. I like it. It suits you." He offered me a hand in rising and walked with me to my room. "Get some sleep. You need anything?"

I shook my head and yawned again, collapsing onto the bed, too tired to bother with changing. A moment later, T's hands were untying and removing my shoes for me as easily as he must have his children's when they were young.

"You don't have to do that," I mumbled.

"No, I don't." He then nudged me to lie in the bed properly and tucked the blankets around me. "Good night."

"Good night."

T kissed the top of my head and left the room, turning off the light and closing the door behind him.

# CHAPTER 23

The following morning, I woke a little before my alarm. I turned it off and climbed out of bed, yawning. Thanks to T's care, I had clothes to change into, so I ambled into the bathroom with my new outfit. T must have still been asleep because the apartment was dark and quiet.

The shower felt amazing, and when I checked my back in the mirror, I realized the wounds there had closed overnight. There was still some tender pink flesh in those places, but that, too, would fade, as would the faint, lingering stiffness in the muscles.

As I considered them, my mind wandered back to Asakku, and I sighed. What was his game? He had to have one, even if it wasn't immediately obvious. Though I supposed his game might not be with me. Excluding this "Hot and Cold" nonsense. As I so often felt, there was a good chance I was nothing but a pawn in a bigger picture.

I brushed my teeth, washed my face, and ran a comb through my short hair. It would need a cut soon, but for now, it was passable. While I didn't put much stock in my appearance, Father John had impressed the importance of good grooming on me. Being clean wasn't something I had ever eschewed, but things like combing my hair seemed like a waste of time.

I dressed in a pair of new jeans, a plain gray t-shirt, and a blue-and-gray flannel that T had said would look good with my eyes. Just after I finished and had put yesterday's clothes in the basket T had loaned me, T's alarm went off in his bedroom. I heard grumbling from behind his door as he woke, growled something unpleasant at his alarm clock, and stretched with a loud groan.

The sounds made me smile some. Despite having only spent two nights here, I already felt more at ease than I had anywhere else. Jim's apartment—as kind as he was to allow me to stay there—had never felt particularly comfortable. First of all, it had been designed for someone in a wheelchair, so I had to hunch or bend at the knees to reach everything. Second, the space was just too tight with the two of us in it.

When T's bedroom door opened, and he lurched toward the bathroom with bleary eyes, Tiny exploded out of the room and charged down the hall at me to put his paws on my shoulders and lick my face. I laughed. "Good morning to you, too."

T took his time in the bathroom, and when he emerged, he was dressed in a clean tank top, flannel shirt, and jeans. He greeted me, then had me help him prepare breakfast for the two of us. Perhaps my mention of knowing nothing about how the world worked had stirred him into the decision that he was to be my mentor in such things.

I did all right, having done plenty of prep cooking while volunteering at the soup kitchen, and T and I made a pair of omelets stuffed with peppers, cheese, and sausage. His was massive, and I'd argued with him until he made mine about a third its size, but he kept shooting me grumpy looks as we ate as though he didn't believe that would be enough to fill me.

When we finished, we both put our plates on the floor and let Tiny lick them clean, both pretending we hadn't. Though when we made eye contact afterward, neither could stop the smile.

We had just finished the dishes when my phone went off with Axton's number on the screen. I picked up. "Good morning."

"You sound awfully chipper," he grumbled, his voice like gravel under a tire.

"I'm sorry." I assumed, given his tone, that 'chipper' was a bad thing to be. Unfortunately, I had no idea what it was, so I couldn't be less.

He sighed, and I heard him take a swig of something. Given what I remembered of his office, I suspected it was coffee. He seemed to drink enough of the stuff that I imagined you could cut him and it would pour out. "You ready to roll? I'll be at your place soon."

"I will be ready, yes."

"See you in five," he said, then hung up.

T was sitting at the table with his own cup of coffee when I passed by him. "Off to save the world?" he asked, giving me a tired smile.

"Well, off to try, at least," I replied, smiling back.

He saluted me with his coffee cup. "Go with God."

I chuckled and nodded. "Technically, everywhere I go is with God. And everywhere you go. And everywhere everyone does. He is everywhere. But… I appreciate your blessing."

When Axton arrived, I was waiting for him in the front hall. I had put my apartment keys on the same key ring as my church keys (which had a little tag on them that displayed a drawing of the church and had the name and address on the back) and clipped them to a belt loop of my pants. I also wore the long coat Asakku had given me. It was, by far, warmer than anything else I owned. Regardless of where the gift had come from, I wasn't so proud as to ignore my own comfort by spurning it.

The snow had stopped overnight, which allowed the plows to do their work. That said, the streets were still a sloppy, wet, icy mess that I was glad I didn't have to sleep on. My mind wandered back to Ether and Maggie, and I said a brief prayer that they were all right before I joined Axton at the car.

He had the heat on high and was drinking what smelled like coffee out of a thermos. Unlike me, I could tell he hadn't slept well. If he'd slept at all. In fact, he was wearing the same clothes he had been the day before. They looked rumpled, like maybe he'd slept in them, but I couldn't tell for sure.

"Right, so with the protests and upcoming renovations, they aren't doing tours, exactly, but I got them to let us explore the church."

"How?" I frowned.

"Being a licensed PI has its benefits. Told 'em I was on a case and that my client said I might find something there. Plus, I made a sizable donation to their renovation fund."

"I'm not sure Jim can afford to —"

Axton cut me off with a shake of his head. "Hammerson's not going to have to pay me for this." Another huge sigh. He seemed to do that a lot. "There are things more important than money, and this is one of 'em. Much as I hate to admit it, this is what I'm best at. And I know Hammerson isn't made of money."

"Thank you." Remembering my conversation with Jim about how the good ones didn't always act good, I smiled a little. Axton was definitely one of the good ones.

As difficult as our interaction was, I knew he was — as I was — driven by doing the right thing for the right reasons.

Axton nodded, and we pulled away from the curb, driving north toward the church.

When we arrived, Axton parked at the side of the road a block or so away. "We'll have to hoof it."

I stared at him blankly. "I do not have hooves."

A snort that might've been laughter left him. "Means walk."

"Oh." I flushed and stepped out of the car. While the snow had ended, the air was bitter cold, and I shivered a little despite my warm coat. Yet again, I found myself grudgingly grateful the demon had given it to me.

Axton followed me out, and the two of us trudged toward the church. As we got closer, the sounds of protest became audible and grew in volume the nearer we got to the building. When we got close enough to see the people protesting, both Axton and I stopped in our tracks, focused on the crowd.

Old North Church is a beautiful colonial church surrounded by modern buildings. It and the campus take up what feels like a city block in the center of downtown Boston. If not for other buildings similar to it in age and placement, it would stick out like a sore thumb, but since Boston has that feel about it, it seems right for the space somehow. It fits. The steeple, historic for its participation in the Revolutionary War, is dwarfed by the massive steel and glass skyscrapers around it, but nonetheless, it stands tall and proud, kept immaculate by the city's conservation efforts.

Right now, however, I was less focused on the beauty of the church and was distracted by a crowd of over a hundred people boiling around the church steps.

"You seeing what I'm seeing?" Axton asked, his voice low.

I nodded. "I am. We are at the right place."

Most of the people protesting were nothing unusual, but sprinkled through the crowd were demons. Some were riding people; others were slinking, invisible to mortal eyes, throughout the gathering, either inspiring them to greater fury or feeding off the emotional energy generated by the crowd. I couldn't tell which for sure.

The two of us watched the protestors seething outside the front doors of the church for a while before Axton pulled out his phone and made a call. When he finished, he put his phone away. "We're going in the back door. Come on. The farther we stay from that, the better."

I nodded, keeping a watchful eye on the crowd as Axton led us around the building to another door, which opened. A tired-looking human woman wearing jeans and a nice blouse gave us a wan smile as she let us into the church.

"I'm sorry about this." Her green eyes were equal parts apologetic and strained.

"It's not your fault, Helen," Axton said, returning her smile. "I have a feeling that half these people don't even really know what they're protesting. Thanks for taking the time."

"Yes, well, I hope you're able to pick up a lead here. Do you need me to show you where things are, or do you mind terribly if I return to my office? This whole mess has been quite a strain on the staff, and I have a lot of work to do." She lingered in the doorway, but her body language screamed that she was in a hurry to get back to whatever we'd pulled her away from.

"You can go. We can handle things from here."

I stepped around Axton and offered the woman my hand. "We are grateful for your help, Helen."

She gave me a quizzical look but shook my hand, which was what I'd hoped she'd do. People liked to shake hands, and not returning the gesture was typically seen as rude, so being "left hanging," as Dust had termed it once, was uncommon. I didn't like when it was done to me, but at that moment, using the social norms of the world to get what I needed done seemed prudent.

I channeled my Grace through my fingers and into her through our contact as we shook hands, and she sighed, some of the strain leaving her. "I'm sorry. I didn't get your name, mister…" She blinked a few times as though seeing me for the first time.

"Cass." I smiled. "Just Cass. I hope your day improves from here." I squeezed her fingers and released her hand.

"Cass. It's nice to meet you. If you need me, I'll be in my office." Helen smiled again, this time more genuine. She then left us alone and retreated down a hallway.

Axton glanced at me once she was out of earshot. "Be careful using that in here."

"It wasn't much," I said, shaking my head. "And this is a church. Where else should I use my Grace?"

"I mean with the horde out front. You'll tip 'em off if we aren't careful." He looked around us and jerked his chin toward a door nearby. "This way."

Axton led us into the sanctuary of the church, which was a beautiful space. Two floors with a full balcony on three sides of the room above. The front of the church, near the massive windows, had a lectern that required the preacher to climb a small, spiral staircase to reach. The wood was dark and old and had been immaculately cared for.

Unlike St. Mary's, which had open pews, Old North had their pews set in boxes, many with plaques hung on the doors. I couldn't fathom the use of such a thing, but right now didn't seem like the time to ask about church architecture.

I walked around the room but paused toward the center as a sensation ran through me from below, as though I were a harp string and someone had plucked me. "It's here," I said, looking at my feet. "Axton, it's here."

Axton approached me and looked down. "Below. I was right. It's in the crypt."

"Isn't it closed for repairs?"

"Yeah. We aren't supposed to go down there."

"Why do I get the feeling that we're going down there anyway?"

"Because you're a smart lady sometimes." He patted my shoulder and walked back toward the front of the church, heading for the lefthand side where a set of stairs led down into the crypt beneath. I followed.

A velvet rope hung across the door with a hastily written sign that said, "No Entry, Repairs Underway, Sorry" with exactly that number of commas. Axton moved one of the small pedestals that held the rope in place to the side.

Beyond it, the door had been left open for, I later learned, air flow. They had fans and dehumidifiers running down there, but any extra air they could get was a bonus.

"Small mercies," Axton said. "The door probably has an alarm on it, so I'm not sure I could've forced it without getting us in trouble."

"Not-so-small mercies. Perhaps this is a sign we are doing the right thing." It certainly felt like one of those odd little "coincidences" that sometimes add up when one is on the correct path. Sometimes, it's as simple as a door being open; other times, it's a street sign flashing the letters "R U O K." The Father has a sense of humor.

Axton grunted and descended the stairs without further word, and I followed. I knew he wouldn't like the idea that he was doing something Heaven had mandated, but at the same time, there was some comfort in knowing it. At least to me.

I noticed the change in temperature first. It was a good ten degrees cooler as we walked down the steps into the crypt. Then the scent hit my nose. It smelled like old mortar, dust, and time. At the base of the stairs, an industrial drying fan was plugged in and blowing, and the sound filled the space, and I heard others going somewhere beyond.

The lighting wasn't uniform, though the area near the stairs was brighter than much of the space beyond. Pipes ran the length of the room, hanging from the ceiling so low, Axton and I had to duck as we slunk toward where we'd both felt the Grace.

The niches all had carved plaques on them featuring various *memento mori* of the time period. This being a church, most were angels, but some of the older ones had willow trees. The depictions were, in my opinion, crude at best, but I had learned that those in the mortal world didn't have much of a concept of how angels looked, so I couldn't fault them.

The space was quiet as though holding its breath and waiting for something. Some of the doors in the crypt hung open, suggesting the occupants of those niches had been moved already, but the one that drew Axton and I to it was still shut.

Unsure of our next move, I looked at Axton in the dim light. A single bulb in a nest of nearby pipes lit the space we were in with uneven shadows, and I squinted at the plaque on the tomb. I didn't recognize the name, but the dates were in the right time.

"Axton, I think this is it."

Then the lights went out.

# CHAPTER 24

I called holy fire to my fingertips, lighting the space better than the light bulb had and earning myself a glare from Axton. "What did I tell you about not tipping our hand?"

"If I can't see down here, I'm going to end up harming myself by walking into something. And we won't be able to get to the—"

A sound cut me off. A quiet grating noise, the sound of stone against stone, and Axton's annoyed expression became surprise and then nervousness. "Hey, you said you were a gate guardian, right?" he asked, his voice tense.

"Yeah...?" I drawled, looking around us and squinting into the deep shadows.

"You, uh, any good with your fists?"

"I'm pass—ow!" Something struck me in the back of the head, and I staggered forward a pace into Axton. "What in the world?"

Axton lashed out and grabbed a small object out of the air, dragging it into the light. A tiny stone angel struggled against his grip, waving its hands and flapping. "This," he said, shaking it, "is a grotesque. Kind of cousins of mine. Sort of. They're church guardians. Should've anticipated th—" He was cut off as another of the little stone angels dive-bombed him. He swatted it away. "Cass, get the nail. I'll keep them off you."

"There are only two. How much trouble could they be?" Another blow struck me, this time in the temple.

"There's a lot more'n two, angel." He looked around us, and I realized he must have been able to see better than I could in the dim lighting.

Rather than arguing with him, I turned back to the niche and felt around the edges of the door, trying to find a way to open it without breaking it outright. Such an act felt disrespectful, and I didn't want to cause more damage to this place than had already been done.

Behind me, I heard the sound of stone impacting stone and glanced in Axton's direction. His skin had hardened and turned the same gray as his eyes usually were. In contrast, his eyes glowed with a faint blue light as he kept the little stone grotesques away from me and either crushed them in his fist or hurled them away into the darkness beyond where I could see.

They didn't seem able to do much damage to him like that, and he was doing a good job keeping them away from me, so I re-focused on my own conundrum.

Eventually, I found a little ridge at the bottom of the stone endcap and tugged at it. While it was wedged firmly in place, I knew if I kept at it, I'd be able to pull it off. I just hoped I could do so without breaking it.

With a silent prayer, I started pulling.

Angels are, by nature, stronger than most mortal creatures. That strength served me well as I manipulated the stone door as best I could. In the end, I managed not to damage it too badly during removal and set the slab aside.

In the niche lay a skeleton wearing the decayed remains of a priest's frock. Time had not been kind to the corpse, but that was the nature of death: to return to the earth and not be as one once was. I had never been this close to a skeleton before, but I ignored the little chill of discomfort. Reaching inside, I tried to disturb the body as little as possible.

There, clasped in the skeleton's hands, was a slender, worn shaft of iron. While it fit the definition of a nail, it more closely resembled a railroad spike in length if not girth, and when my fingers brushed it, the shock of Grace through me was almost too much for me to handle. I flinched a little.

"Hurry up!" Axton said behind me, his voice strained.

I took a breath and grabbed the nail, gently withdrawing it from the skeletal fingers. Some scared part of me wondered if the hands would lash out and grab me, but no such thing happened. When I touched the nail, it felt like gripping into a live wire. Power thrummed through my arm and vibrated through me, resonating through every fiber of my being, causing all of me to sit up and take notice at once. I withdrew the nail and replaced the stone I'd dislodged. I wedged it in place to the best of my ability and then turned toward Axton. "I've got it."

"Great. Now let's get out of here." He shattered the last of the creatures diving at him and whipped out a burgundy cloth bag with gold lettering spelling out "Royal Crown" printed on it. "Wrap it in this, and let's go."

I did as he told me to do and stuffed the nail into my coat pocket just as the sound of more rocks sliding around in the darkness hit my ears. "Uh, Axton? What's that?"

"Nope. That's what that is. A big nope. A whole heaping mound of it, in fact." He shooed me toward the door as the sound grew louder and became stomping footsteps behind us.

"That's a much bigger nope than the little ones were," I said over my shoulder as I ducked and weaved through the pipes, though in my distraction, I walked straight into one with a loud *clang*.

My head reverberated like a bell, and I stopped to try and collect my thoughts. Axton grabbed the back of my jacket and dragged me along with him in his rush. As I blinked and tried to refocus my eyes, I could see something big stomping after us in the darkness. The light of my holy fire barely reached it, but from what I could see, the shattered remains of the tiny grotesques had reformed into something far bigger. Nearly ogre-sized and unbothered by the low pipes and duct work, it chased after us, the faces of the destroyed angels staring at us with empty, accusing eyes.

He'd been right. That was a whole lot of nope.

Despite Axton's edict not to use my Grace, I didn't see a whole lot of options. Instead of running, I reached into my pocket and withdrew the nail, pulling it out of the bag.

"Cassiel, what are you—" Axton started to say, but I cut him off with action.

Drawing on some of the vast well of power the nail contained, I pulled it into me, which caused the holy fire I'd called to my hands to blaze like the sun, driving away every inch of shadow in the basement. I'd barely even scratched the surface of the power this relic held, and already I felt close to what I remembered my full angelic strength to be.

No longer particularly concerned by the hulking mass of stone fueled by magic, I took a few steps toward it, leaning to the side a little as it swung a hulking fist toward my head. The stone hand breezed by my skin, missing by less than an inch. I had calculated it that way. The extra

Grace imparted faster reflexes and more perfect perception of my surroundings, which gave me the ability to time things with far more precision.

Once the fist had passed, I took a step forward and punched the creature in its center mass with the hand holding the nail. It functioned a little like a set of brass knuckles in that it kept my knuckles in alignment as I struck the unyielding surface.

The creature exploded into the shattered remains of the various grotesques that had combined to create it which, I hoped, would give us time to escape. If the grotesques were lesser cousins to the gar, then likely they were down here to protect the crypt somehow. Perhaps the renovations had disturbed them, or they maybe somehow sensed our intent to remove something that we had no business removing. Or maybe the demons' Blight outside had made them a little more murder-y than usual. I couldn't tell.

But what I did know was that I felt *good*.

Axton and I hurried out of the basement with an unspoken understanding between us, and he closed the heavy security door behind us. For all the good that would do if the grotesquenstein monster reassembled itself and decided to follow.

I put the nail back into its bag and stuffed it into my pocket again, still thrumming with Grace. "Grotesques, huh?" I asked, looking Axton's way.

Axton grunted. "Yep." I noticed his eyes were glowing again, likely reflecting the power the nail had produced and the Grace I had used.

"So the church made little stone monsters to wreak havoc on things?"

"Well, this church did."

"Those seemed more irritating than anything," I said.

"Would've been more than that if we were anything less equipped than what we are. Some of those little bastards hit pretty hard."

Given the developing ache in my skull from the bruises they'd left me, I had to agree. He had a point. They probably hadn't been trying to defend the relic from things like us anyway. Perhaps they hadn't been there to protect the relic at all and had been just guardians of the dead.

"Well, I've got the nail," I said, patting my pocket. "Now we just need to figure out what we're going to do with it."

"First thing we have to do with it is get out of the church without the demons realizing what we've done, but... I'm guessing that's too much to ask. They'd have felt it moving and probably sensed the grotesques in action. So they'll be on high alert."

Something hit one of the windows of the sanctuary, and I frowned in that direction. Another blow struck the window, this time breaking out some of the glass, and a rock the size of my fist landed in one of the pews.

I rose, my hand sliding back into my coat pocket to grip the nail in my fist. Even through the cloth, I could feel it humming, its Grace reaching out to my own. The air felt electric. Tight. I could almost see the threads of tension. Somewhere down in my gut, I knew something bad was about to happen.

When I met Axton's eyes, I could tell he felt the same. Neither of us spoke, unwilling to break the moment of calm before whatever came. He nodded to me, his expression calm as he put his hand on my shoulder and squeezed. Whatever came, we were in this together. If not friends, at least allies.

The first Molotov cocktail sailed through the air and struck the wood, splattering gasoline across the carpet. Flames leapt upward from the accelerant and caught on the fabric.

A second cocktail followed, breaking through a different window. Then a third from another part of the sanctuary.

"Why the hell isn't the fire suppression system coming on?" Axton snarled, looking around at the spreading flames. Then he shook his head. "The power. They've done something to the grid. Probably the water, too. They're trying to drive us out since they can't come in."

"We need to get Helen and get out of here," I said, watching the flames spread. It reminded me of when I'd first met Codiel, though this time, I wasn't bleeding to death.

"First things first." Axton glanced at me and grimaced before he took a slow, deep breath.

# CHAPTER 25

Gargoyles, the statues around cathedrals that act as drain spouts, must have been either a nod to or a mockery of gar. I learned this when Axton opened his mouth. A steady gout of water erupted from him, splashing over the places the fire had caught and misting heavily enough in the air that it smothered the flames. He turned in a slow circle, putting out the fires as he went. Sure, the sanctuary was drenched and parts of it had been damaged by the fire, but at least the whole building wasn't at risk. At least this second. There was nothing stopping them from trying again. Fire, after all, wasn't the hardest thing to come by.

"We need to get out of here," I said, my mind spinning as I tried to figure out the best answer.

"I've got an idea," Axton said with a fierce grin, his eyes awash with blue light still. "Those demons are after the nail, right? Probably able to sniff it out because of the Grace."

I nodded.

"I need to borrow as much of your Grace as you can without keeling over. We imbue me with it, and I go out the front. Most demons aren't that smart. They'll sense the power and chase me. It might not get all of them, but it should cause enough that you might be able to slip out the back."

As far as plans went, it depended a lot more on luck than I wished it did, but it was better than nothing. "We can try it." The idea concerned me since, if I gave him that much of my Grace—even with it having been bolstered by the nail—I might not have enough to face off against anything nasty not lured by Axton's ploy without drawing from the nail again, which would shatter any illusions of the nail being elsewhere. But of the two of us, he was probably the more durable, and the ruse would definitely draw a lot of attention.

"You ready for this?" Axton asked.

I nodded. "As ready as I expect I can be."

"All right. Charge me up, then make for the back door. Once the chaos starts, get out of here."

"What about Helen?"

"She's either hiding in her office, or she got out of here already. Either way, she's probably safer wherever she is. Besides, once we get the demons out of here, the riot should die down. And I expect the cops will be here in a few minutes."

I sighed but nodded. He was right. We didn't have much time, and once we diverted the demonic attention from this place, Helen would probably be safe enough. Without the demonic intervention, the crowd's fury would probably break pretty quickly, and I had a feeling most of them would be pretty confused about what they were even angry *about*.

I put my hand on Axton's shoulder, and he nodded to me, taking a shuddering breath. Then I poured my Grace into him, filling him. He drew it in like air into lungs, a deep breath long forgotten. The blue of his eyes glowed brighter and brighter until it was almost the shining brilliance of holy fire.

A larger portion of my Grace had been restored after the fight with the drug-dealing demon whose name I'd never learned, but it was still barely a fraction of the power I'd once wielded. That said, even a fraction of the power of a seraph is no small thing.

Fatigue washed over me, and I dropped my hand from Axton's shoulder while he let out a rumbling growl. "Get to the back door," he said, his voice resonating deeper in his chest as he rolled his shoulders and stretched as though waking up after a long sleep.

I didn't argue and jogged out of the sanctuary to the door we'd come in by, praying that I had the energy and strength to do this. Once I left the church and was certain I wasn't being followed, I'd figure out what to do with the nail, but the first step was getting out of there. Or, as Dust would have said, "getting the hell out of Dodge."

I had no idea what the saying meant, but it felt apt.

As we'd agreed, I stood by the back door. A few moments later, there was some crashing, followed by heavy footfalls charging across the sanctuary. The front doors burst open, and all hell broke loose outside. I had no idea what exactly was happening, but it certainly sounded like the chaos Axton had told me to wait for. Taking that as my cue, I opened the door and stepped out.

I didn't see what happened exactly. There was just a rush, a body pressed up against mine, and something sharp at my throat.

"Hello, dear angel." Asakku's voice was in my ear, and warmth flooded me from behind from the contact.

I should have expected it. Should have known better. I didn't trust him to begin with, after all, but that didn't stop the sharp pang that pierced through me when I realized what was happening.

I sighed, the edge of the knife pressing harder into my skin as I did but not breaking it. Which I was grateful for; I'd seen what it had done to the demons he'd used the blade on in the park. "I should've known."

"It's more complicated than that. But yes, I do really need the relic in your pocket. We can fight over it, but in the end, I've got you in a very compromised position, and we both know how the fight would end. I would," he hissed in a breath, "*really* prefer not to kill you, but I will if I must."

He was right, and I knew it. Tears stung my eyes. "Why? What is this even for?" I asked.

His voice came out surprisingly pained. "I can't tell you. Even if I wanted to, I can't. If it helps, deceiving you brought me no pleasure."

"Oh, well, good for you." I swallowed hard as his hand reached into my coat pocket and pulled out the Royal Crown bag by the strings holding it shut. He very carefully put it into his suit coat. "I'm sorry I'm no fun."

"I didn't say that, Cassiel. I said deceiving you brought me no pleasure."

His voice lacked the triumph I expected. The sick, twisted amusement. The glee. Instead, he sounded solemn and worried. Almost apologetic if he could have managed it. "I'll be in touch soon."

Then he was gone, as if he'd never been there. The only thing remaining was the faintest scent of brimstone and some kind of cologne I couldn't identify.

I sagged against the wall, my fingers curling into fists. *Idiot. Fool. Moron.* A dozen or so pejorative words flooded through my mind in reference to myself. Axton was going to be furious. As well he should be. Jim would be disappointed. I didn't even want to think about what Codiel might think of me.

The cold wind froze the tears on my cheeks. Or at least it felt like it had. I didn't have long. I needed to get out of there before the horde realized it had been duped and came back. And before the police arrived.

It took all my effort to straighten up from the wall as the fatigue from charging Axton like I had hit me like a truck, magnified by the sense of hopelessness roaring through my chest. The presence of the nail must have been masking just how much of my own Grace I'd given Axton, and in its absence, I felt like an empty cup.

"Damn you, Asakku," I said quietly. "Damn you."

I took one step, then another, and managed to stagger away from the church and into the winding streets around the building. I didn't know where I was going or how I was going to get home with how exhausted I felt. I didn't know where Axton had gone. And at that moment, I didn't care.

Lacking any other sort of motivation or logic, I walked until I couldn't anymore and sunk down onto a bench near a bus stop, burying my head in my hands.

# CHAPTER 26

"You must be cold."

I recognized the voice and turned my head to look at Codiel, who sat beside me on the bench, unbothered by the chill in his robe and sandals. "I'm sorry," I said, not sure I could say anything else. What else could I say?

"For being cold?" He tilted his head, his long fall of golden hair slipping off his shoulder. "That is a silly thing to apologize for, Cassiel."

"No, for…" I trailed off. "You know what for."

"Oh, my sister." He rested his hand on my back, and warmth poured from his fingers, filling me like the cocoa T had given me the night before. Moreso, even. "You say that as if you have failed."

"But the nail—"

Codiel cut me off. "—did not go to the demon seeking it. Well, the one you were trying to foil."

"I do not understand. Asakku, he…" My throat closed against the words. I didn't know why I felt such an acute sense of betrayal. I'd known from the start that he was playing me. So why did it hurt so much?

"Sitting out here alone in the snow will not solve your problems, sister. You should return home and rest."

"I don't think I have the strength to go that far right now."

"Mm." Codiel considered me a moment. "While my ability to interfere is limited, I suppose bearing you home would not be *too* much involvement. Shall I carry you there?"

My pride warred with my fatigue until the fatigue won. "If you wouldn't mind."

"If I minded, would I have offered? You are quite silly, Cassiel." He laughed, the sound ringing out like bells on a clear day. "Come, my weary sister." He stood and, with no effort at all, lifted me into his arms. I must have weighed no more than a feather to him for how he handled me. A moment later, we were airborne.

While he could have probably just teleported us to the apartment building, he chose to fly for whatever reason. Though the flight gave me more time to think. Perhaps that was his intent. I buried my head in Codiel's neck and closed my eyes as he carried me, reliving the events of the last hour.

If Asakku hadn't been behind the whole thing and orchestrated it from the beginning, who had? Was this some kind of demonic political fight? Perhaps whoever had started this was someone Asakku detested. Or perhaps he wanted the power for himself.

Though what he'd do with it, I couldn't really figure out. Grace like that would be toxic to him—or to any demon. It was too potent, too clear, and too powerful for them to handle it. He'd barely been able to touch the bag the nail was in.

Was it for some kind of ritual? Was he storing it to give it to someone else? Maybe a creature in service to the demons but not a demon themselves?

Codiel alighted on the sidewalk outside T's apartment and set me upright. "There you are."

"Thank you, brother," I said, shoving my hands in my pockets, abruptly aware that the coat I wore had come from the demon who had just betrayed me. "I appreciate the ride."

The brilliant smile he gave me could have melted the snow. "While I am allowed very little leave to act on your behalf, the occasional aid is probably not pushing the bounds of my purview too much. Do try to get some rest."

He vanished, but as I walked inside, a set of footprints appeared in the snow beside me, reminding me I wasn't alone. My throat tightened a little. Codiel was kind in ways his purview didn't call him to be. After all, watchers aren't much supposed to interact with their charges. He'd gone out of his way to show me mercy beyond his station and remind me that Heaven hadn't forsaken me entirely. No matter how it felt at times.

I fumbled my keys into my hand and opened the front door, heading inside. Once in the apartment, I realized T must've still been at work and checked the time. It was barely past noon. I felt ragged and sunk down onto the couch, draping an arm over my eyes.

I had just dozed off when my phone rang. "Yes?"

"Cassiel." It was Axton. "How're things looking?"

"I… uh…" I didn't know how to tell him.

"Don't you fucking tell me," he growled. "What did you do, drop it in the Charles?"

My throat tightened. "No, I… The demon who told us where to find it. He caught me outside the church and took the nail."

I had never heard that many curse words all strung together, many of them accounting for physical impossibilities I had trouble imagining. "Why didn't you smite him?"

"He… what is the phrase." I scowled, dredging my mind for the various expressions I'd learned since I'd fallen. "He jumped me. I didn't have the chance. Besides, he's an archdemon, and I used almost all of my Grace on that ploy you came up with. There was nothing I could do to fight him, and it would have been suicide. He would have killed me and taken it anyway. At least this way, I'm alive and have a chance of getting it back."

More swearing. It went on for a good few minutes, getting weirder and weirder and starting to involve languages other than English. "Fine. Just… fine. We found it once. We can find it again. We know who has it. If we have a trail, we can get it back." It sounded to me like Axton was more telling himself that than telling me.

"I have no idea where he went with it." I sighed and leaned into the couch cushions. "Or why."

Axton took a long, slow breath through his nose and exhaled it through his mouth. I could hear the sound over the line, and I recognized it as one of the various techniques Jim had taught me for controlling my emotions. "I'm going to circle back to the church and see if I can find anything. Where are you?"

"Home."

"All right. Give me a few hours, and I'll come by, and we can talk."

I didn't want to wait that long, but I didn't see any other options. I agreed, and we rang off, leaving me alone in the silence of the apartment.

Well, mostly alone. Tiny must have heard me come in and talk things over with Axton because he trotted down the hall from T's bedroom and licked my face until I laughed and shoved him away. He sat in front of me, his tail hitting the floor with rhythmic thumps, and put his head on my knee, eventually nudging my arm until I patted him.

Not sure what else to do, I turned on the television and tried to ignore the jangling anxiety. I couldn't do anything about the nail now. I had no way to hunt down Asakku, either, given that I knew he'd not given me his real name.

Knowing an angel's—or demon's— name provides power. It's not the same kind as can be exercised over the fae or other such beings, and our names typically come in multiple forms and spellings across time. My own name, for example, has been written many ways by those of the world: Cassiel, Qafsi'el, Kasfiyail, Cafziel, Cafzyel and many more. They're all mostly correct and contain the same sounds, more or less, as my name in Enochian, but none are truly my name. I use Cassiel because it's the closest, but I wouldn't give my true name out so carelessly. They are jealously guarded things since, with a true name, an angel or demon may be summoned and bound. Our true names are also typically represented as sigils rather than words, so you can't just say it out loud and demand we show. There's a process.

Most angels don't know one another's true names with the exception of some of the chroniclers, who often know everyone's. That's their job, however. Watcher angels, like Codiel, often know the true names of their charges (assuming they have one) and can use it to locate and keep an eye on the ones they are overseeing.

In this case, however, I only knew Asakku had once been an angel because the degree of Blight he wielded was too great for him to be anything but an archdemon. That, however, was all I knew. Had I known his name, I might have been able to hunt down his sigil, but he'd given me no such avenue.

As I said, too smart for that.

I flipped through channels and settled on the news since it had become something of a familiar thing to me. A female centaur was acting as anchor, standing outside in a park. Her human skin was a rich brown, nearly bronze, and paired well with the chestnut coat her horse half carried. "Correct, Todd. While there's been a reduction in street incidents involving the drug known as 'Ripper' since last autumn, cases involving it have begun to rise again this winter."

We had destroyed the demon responsible for it, hadn't we? I scowled and paused in my patting, leaning forward and turning up the volume, my focus now entirely on the screen.

"Thank you, Cora," another voice said, and the screen shifted to a man in a newsroom. Todd, I guessed. "Authorities aren't sure what has caused the fluctuation in presence in the drug, but communities across New England are starting to report more of it on their streets with incidents involving Ripper happening as far away as L.A., California. Next, we have the weather. Word on the street is we have a nor'easter blowing in overnight with temperatures in the—"

I'd stopped listening by then. I didn't know where California was beyond a vague notion of it being several thousand miles to the west of Boston. I thought we had put a stop to the flow of Ripper when we'd stopped the demon producing it, but there must have been others. Which meant it was a bigger plot than just an attempt to cause local trouble. The notion made my blood run cold.  ·

Worse, I didn't know where the connection was. Was this all part of something bigger? Something more dangerous? Or was I seeing things that didn't exist? I had no way to know, and that awareness of just how much I was missing of whatever the big picture was left me nauseatingly anxious.

# CHAPTER 27

Axton arrived, and I went down to let him in, steeling myself for his reaction to having lost the nail. It wasn't going to be pretty, I expected, but there was no getting around it. One way or another, we had to figure out what to do next, and that meant talking to him. I couldn't hide in the apartment forever.

I met him at the door. "Come upstairs. You must be as tired as I am," I said by way of invitation. Also, it meant the discussion would be somewhat more private.

Axton's expression was hard, and his eyes were furious, but he nodded and followed me up to T's door. I let him in, and Tiny trotted over, sniffing at him. The big dog took his time before he seemed to accept Axton. Despite his rage and frustration, he gave Tiny several thumps to the side. I had come to recognize the gesture since T often did it, and Tiny seemed to appreciate the contact.

Tiny leaned up to lick Axton's face, making him sputter with minor annoyance, but he continued patting until Tiny dropped down and padded off into the living room. I followed and gestured to Axton to sit. He took T's usual spot while I perched on the edge of the couch, resting my elbows on my knees and fidgeting, unsure what to do with my hands.

Neither of us spoke for a long while before Axton sighed and shook his head. "No use blaming yourself for it. You handed most of your Grace off to me, and then I took off running with it. Our ploy didn't quite work the way we'd hoped, and we got outsmarted. As much as we both want to blame you for it, it doesn't make sense to. He's an archdemon, and he played us both like a piano." He growled the last words, clenching his fists, but he relaxed them a moment later. "All that's left is to find him before he does something terrible with the relic."

I replayed my conversations with Asakku over and over in my mind, trying to put it together. Certainly, everything could have been a ploy, but something in my gut whispered that not everything had been. I tried to ignore it, to dismiss it, but the little voice lingered. I'd been taken advantage of before in almost the same way. A demon convincing me he was harmless and using that to...

"Damn it all to hell," I said, my throat tight. "Just... just damn it." I had never sworn before, outside repeating things others had said, but this circumstance seemed to call for it. It felt like the thing to do.

"You got that right." Axton rubbed his hands over his head. "Is there anything at all that you can tell me about him that you haven't yet?"

Despite everything, I sighed. "When he took it, he seemed almost apologetic. He said he didn't want to kill me, for whatever *that* is worth, and said he'd be in touch soon."

Axton laughed bitterly. "Well, that's helpful."

I felt similar, but I didn't have anything to say for it. The apologetic, worried expression on his face filled my mind's eye. It was possible that he was an incredible actor. There was no reason for me to think otherwise, but at the same time, that tug in my chest wouldn't go away. Fool me once, shame on you. Fool me twice, shame on me. I couldn't trust it. I'd already had my feelings twisted against me in this same way before I'd fallen. Arazael had spent far longer on the con, however, before twisting the knife. Asakku? As far as long cons went, a week or so of interaction was a weak one.

So why did I keep seeing the apology in his eyes? The worry? Why did I have this hollow ache?

My phone went off, capturing my attention. The caller ID told me it was from Eirlas, so I took a slow breath and answered, trying to set aside the disaster that had been my morning.

"Hello?"

"Hey, Cass. It's Eirlas." He sounded a little shaken.

"My phone told me so. What's wrong?"

"Father Demoyne just told Dust and I we are no longer needed at the shelter and kitchen, so—"

My growl cut him off. "He *what*?"

"We kind of knew it was coming. I just wanted to tell you in advance so you wouldn't—"

"Are you still near the church?"

"No. He did it over the phone, but—"

"I'm going to have a conversation with him."

"Jesus, Cass," Eirlas said, his tone moving from the edge of tears to frustration. "Can you let me get a sentence out?"

"Sorry." I tried to rein in my temper as I stood up and began to pace. I could feel Axton's and Tiny's eyes on me.

"What I was going to say was that Dust, me, and Jim are going over there to talk to him, and I wanted you to come with us. Nobody knows the scriptures like you do. While he doesn't listen pretty much ever, I wanted to try and convince him to change his mind."

I nodded, then realized he couldn't see me over the phone. "I'm on my way. I'll meet you there."

"Thanks. I doubt it'll make a difference, but we have to try."

"Agreed."

We rang off, and I put my phone in my pocket. "I need to go to the church. There's a situation happening."

"This related to the whole demon situation?"

"No. Father Demoyne is trying to force my friends out of the church because they are gay, and he foolishly believes the scripture says anything about that. I am going to have a word with him. Again. I am likely to be thrown out of the church as well, but..."

Axton sighed heavily. "I'll come with. I know something about the way the church works. Who is this guy, anyway?"

"I do not know." With my stress and frustration, the contractions fell out of my speech. "The church sent him after Father John died."

"I see. Look, uh, you remember that woman I introduced you to? Ruth?"

I nodded.

"She knows the bishop pretty well. I think she'd probably be furious about what's happening here. When your conversation today goes up in flames, we can call her."

# CHAPTER 28

Jim's van was in the parking lot when we arrived at the church, and Eirlas and Dust stood near it, talking to him. I stepped out of Axton's car and walked over with Axton shadowing me. Jim greeted us first. "Cass, Axton." He then looked at the others. "Axton's an old acquaintance of mine. He's working with Cass on the whole... demon situation."

Dust, who had his arm around Eirlas's shoulders, gave Axton a quick nod. Eirlas looked like he'd been crying. "Hey."

Axton returned it but said nothing.

"So, what is the plan?" I asked, crossing my arms. The adrenaline and emotions of the failure of my plan, the betrayal, the frustration, had all congealed into a burning lump of fury in the pit of my stomach. One I was fully prepared to unleash on Father Demoyne.

Eirlas leaned further into Dust and sighed. "I don't know exactly. Go in there and try and make him change his mind?"

Dust grunted and shook his head, kissing the top of Eirlas's head, holding the smaller man closer to his chest. "The work there is important to both of us. All of us. We've done a lot to help the people who come here, and we aren't willing to just walk away. Because you know the moment we do, that rat bastard will gut all the programs we've been working on. He started it just after he arrived."

Heads nodded. We all remembered Father Demoyne more or less kicking me out of the church, stopping the breakfast service at the soup kitchen, and starting to limit the work of the other programs the church had for the homeless. He claimed that they hadn't been properly approved through the diocese. That was, of course, just a cover for him not wanting to associate with those kinds of people. He'd also been cracking down on the drug and alcohol groups that met there, moving their time slots around and making it harder and harder for them to meet.

Jim had talked to me about it endlessly since he was in charge of managing the small groups there and had been fighting this for the last year.

"Right." I cracked my knuckles.

Jim put his hand on my arm and squeezed. "Don't hit him."

"I didn't plan to."

"Or anything else."

"Fine." I hadn't intended to strike anything. I respected that building and its place in my life too much. For all Father Demoyne had done damage, it was still my first home in this world. It was where I had met Father John, Jim, Dust, and Eirlas. It was where I had learned how to live in the world. As tempting as it was to grab Father Demoyne and haul him out by his ears, I knew it wouldn't work that way. Though I very much wanted to remind him of exactly what angels were capable of. He didn't know I was one, but maybe it was time he found out.

"All right, so, we are going to meet with him in his office. Cassiel obviously knows the most about scripture, so she can argue any points of that he brings up." Jim looked up at me for confirmation, and I nodded.

"I can recite it to him in the original languages if I need to."

Jim smiled a little. "I'm not sure that will be necessary since I doubt he speaks them."

Axton cleared his throat. "I, uh, I know I'm not really part of this, but I know a lot about how the church works if you need backup. Or I can just wait outside. Whatever you need."

Jim smiled a little at him. "I'm not sure there will be room for all of us in his office as it is, but you're welcome to stand around looking intimidating if you want to. You're good at it."

The two chuckled as if sharing some kind of inside joke before Jim turned his attention to Eirlas and Dust. "The two of you can bring up how much work you've done to serve the community and the hours of service you've provided. Also, you can talk about how the shelter and kitchen would collapse without you both because, well, they would, and I think we all know it."

"What about you?" I asked, tilting my head.

"I'm just going to sit there and look righteous unless I need to open my mouth."

"Fair enough."

With all of our roles assigned, our little squadron entered the church through the sanctuary, moving to the back of the room and then into the small office off to the side of it. As we approached the door, images of Father John's murder rolled through my mind. I could almost smell the coppery scent of blood. The sulfur. The brimstone. My stomach tightened, and I had to take a deep breath to avoid being sick. I hadn't been in there more than a handful of times since Father John's death, but it never seemed to get easier.

Father Demoyne, a pinch-faced elf who managed to make even his race's supernatural beauty look ugly, was sitting behind his desk, hunched over something he was writing. He lifted his head when Jim entered and opened his mouth to speak, but the rest of us filled the cramped space before he got any words out.

He snapped his mouth shut, teeth meeting with a click. His mild gray eyes heated with fury, and he stared daggers at Jim, who gave him the most polite, empty smile I had ever seen. He didn't show it often, but I knew Jim could be terrifying under the right circumstances. He'd been a Marine for a long time, after all, and had a rod of iron where his spine should be.

Metaphorically speaking. See? I can use them too.

"Father Demoyne, it came to my attention that you intended on firing Dust and Eirlas from their positions at the shelter and kitchen. That leaves me in a bit of a bind in the manpower arena. I was hoping you could be convinced to allow them to continue their work." Jim's voice had this eerie quality of being so polite, it had the opposite effect. I'd have to ask him sometime how he did it.

Father Demoyne's mouth thinned so much, I could have sworn it nearly vanished before he spoke. "There is nothing to discuss. I told these two that their sinful relationship had no place in this—"

My mouth moved faster than my brain. "Their relationship is not sinful. Your judgment of it is," I snarled.

"The scriptures are clear on—"

"Oh, *are they?*" I said, moving through the small group and placing both my hands on his desk, leaning forward. At six feet tall, broad, and bearing all the intensity of a warrior of Heaven, I am quite capable of being intimidating when I want to be. And I very much wanted to be. "Do tell."

Father Demoyne shrunk back in his chair a bit but pulled himself together. "Genesis nineteen—"

"—was about an attempt to rape two angels. Which was a horrific breach of the laws of hospitality. Try again."

"That is not at all clear in—"

A noise that was probably closer to a growl left me, cutting him off. "Were you there? Did you talk to the angels in question?"

"Of course not. You can't mean to claim that—"

"Oh, I do. And I am. My brothers did not care about people who have inclination toward one gender or another. They struck those people down because they were trying to do them egregious harm and were acting with malice in their hearts. Furthermore, their entire culture was centered around vices to the point where they ignored the needs of the poor and outcast in direct violation of—"

"Cassiel," Jim said, his tone sharp.

I straightened, accidentally knocking over a pen holder and scattering writing implements across Father Demoyne's desk.

"This is heresy. I will not stand for it!" Father Demoyne barked in what I am sure he thought was a very imposing manner. Though the squeak in his voice betrayed him. "I will have you excommunicated!"

It was the wrong thing to do, but I couldn't help it. I burst out laughing. "You have no authority over me."

Axton elbowed me in the ribs sharp enough to shut me up. "You're not helping." He said the words out of the corner of his mouth before he shoved me backward and took my place. "Look, uh... Father Whatever-Your-Name-Is, what Cassiel was trying to say—badly—is that you don't have the right to do that. You know, and I know, that the church wrestled with all of that centuries ago when trying to decide whether to accept dryads and dwarves into the church. They concluded that condemning on the basis of sexuality doesn't make much sense when there are creatures on this earth who reproduce with pollen or even without sex at all. Look at gnomes!" Axton's tone had that same, calm quality Jim's did. "We all know that the *Lex Sexualis* of 1128 embraced creatures whose reproduction had nothing to do with male and female and saw it as unfair to apply edicts relating to sexuality to any race if it could not be applied to all. As such, any opinions you might have on the matter are rendered inoperable under church law."

Father Demoyne's face turned first red and then purple, and he sputtered, but no full words or sentences came out.

"Furthermore, depriving the shelter and soup kitchen of their managers without naming adequate replacements or with having any just cause also violates their civil rights under equal employment doctrine. The church has had a lot of bad press over the years for this kind of thing." He sucked a breath in through his teeth. "It could get messy if the press found out. I'm sure the bishop would *love* to hear about it."

"They're volunteers. It doesn't violate the EEOC," Father Demoyne shot back.

Axton shrugged. "It would still look pretty bad in the press."

Eirlas cleared his throat. "Look, Father Demoyne, with all due respect, we've been serving this community for a long time. The people here know us, and the programs we run and services we provide are very important to this neighborhood. 'Contribute to the needs of God's people, and welcome strangers into your home.' That's what we do here, and we've helped a lot of people who needed it."

Dust took Eirlas's hand and squeezed it. "He's right. I've donated thousands to the church over the years and done a lot of the work myself to help avoid needing to pay for repairs. That kitchen exists as it does because of the work I put into it. It isn't fair or right to kick us out just because you don't like our relationship. Besides, if it *is* a problem, that's between us and God. Not you."

Father Demoyne ground his teeth. "All of you out. Go! Except you." He jabbed a finger in Jim's direction.

Jim raised a brow and tilted his head just a little but said nothing. I recognized the set of his jaw and expression in his eyes and knew he was going to spit fire at Father Demoyne the moment the door closed.

Axton grabbed my shoulder and hauled me out of the room. Dust and Eirlas followed, and we shut the door behind us. "What the hell were you thinking?" he hissed. "Just going to pop your wings out and go all righteous fury on the man? Huh? You think that would've solved anything?" Axton jabbed a finger into my chest to punctuate his words. "You. Aren't. Helping."

I pulled away from him and left the sanctuary through a side door that led into the courtyard between the various church buildings and walked across the yard to sit on one of the benches scattered around the space. No one followed. Letting my anger get the better of me had been a mistake, and it was one that could have screwed things up for two of the people I cared about most. It didn't matter that I was having a bad day; they deserved better of me.

The wind picked up, and I glanced at the sky, noticing the weather was changing. Dark, heavy clouds had rolled in, threatening snow. Or rain. Maybe both. I wasn't good enough at telling the weather to know for sure. But it felt cold enough to snow. "What the hell do you want from me?" I yelled. "Why isn't my best good enough?"

Silence answered.

# CHAPTER 29

I didn't really pay attention to how long I sat out there, but when Dust sat down next to me on the bench, I realized the light had shifted. He didn't say anything at first and just shoved a disposable coffee cup filled with something hot into my hands. The cold hadn't really registered until that moment, but as warmth flooded my hands, I could tell I'd been outside too long.

"You didn't screw up our chances," he said quietly. "Axton said he's got a friend who will talk to the bishop for us, and so did Jim. Honestly," a smile curled one corner of his mouth, "I kind of liked seeing you tear into him like that. It felt good knowing you had our back in there."

I didn't know how to reply, so I just nodded. I hadn't drunk any of what he'd given me yet, but the warmth felt good on my fingers. For now, it was enough.

"I know it has to be frustrating for you. You know the truth of all of this. Religion, I mean. Seeing people like him who are using it to hurt others has to drive you crazy."

"Yes." I nodded. "The truth is bigger than any of you know. It's not about all these little rules you've made up. Not a one of you really has it right. Christians, Jews, Muslims, Shinto, Buddhists… All of you have pieces. It falls apart at the places where you start trying to guess what the Father wants rather than just listening. 'God is love.' That is really all you need to know. Love, kindness, compassion, mercy, generosity… Those are what matter. The rest is just window dressing. And yet you fight wars over it. Kill each other."

I sighed. "If Jesus walked the earth today, Father Demoyne would have excommunicated *Him*."

Dust nodded. "I know you've got a whole lot going on right now. With the whole demons business, I mean. It… it means a lot that you'd stop by to yell at Father Demoyne for us."

"How could I not?" I said, finally lifting my head. My back complained a little, the muscles stiff from having been in one position so long. "You're my friends. The family I was given when I fell."

Dust put a hand to my shoulder, squeezing tightly. "I'm glad to know you, Cass."

A deep sigh tore out of me, and I returned my gaze to the ground. "I failed my mission today. The demons got the relic. I just wish I knew what they wanted it for."

"Well," Dust said, sitting back some and looking up at the drifting snow, "if everything is God's plan, doesn't that mean this was, too?"

I didn't have an answer for that one.

"Could you have done better or different?"

"I don't think so."

"In that case, you did everything you could to do what you thought was right, and it still didn't work out. You weren't lazy or foolish. You weren't careless. Sometimes, bad things happen. They sometimes even happen to good people. It might not make sense to us, but we're not meant to know."

"That doesn't make it feel less like I have failed."

"My point is that sometimes, it happens. That's life, Cass. You remember when I got possessed?"

I nodded.

"Was that some kind of failure on my part? Was it my fault?"

"Of course not. There's nothing you could have done."

Dust raised his eyebrows at me.

"...Oh."

"Drink your cocoa. You'll get hypothermia if you stay out in the cold too long." He brushed snow off my back and shoulders and stood up. "Eirlas and I are going to head home, but I wanted to thank you for sticking up for us."

"You're welcome." I had some of the cocoa, able to feel the trail of heat from my lips down into my chest where it sat and radiated out through the rest of me.

Dust took a few steps and paused before looking back at me. "Don't be so hard on yourself, Cass. Missions go sideways. Jim and I? We know that better'n anyone. No matter what you do, sometimes it just doesn't work. When that happens, the only answer is to keep pushing forward. You can't go backward, so sitting around hating yourself for it doesn't fix the problem."

He tromped off toward the door to the kitchen which, I realized, was where he'd come from.

"He's right, you know."

I froze as Asakku's voice hit my ears. Not sure where he was or what he wanted, I took a slow, deep breath and tried to quell the instinct to attack him. It wouldn't go well. But that didn't stop me from wanting to gut him. I struggled to not crush the cup I held, instead forcing myself to take a sip of my drink. "What do you want?" The words came out as cold and unfriendly as I felt.

"I told you I'd be back."

"You aren't welcome here."

"I never was." He grinned, walking into my line of sight and standing a little out of arm's reach. A smart tactical choice. I would have grabbed him and snapped his neck if I could. "I wanted to explain."

"As if anything you say is the truth?" I finished my cocoa and stood, anger infusing my chilled limbs with new life. "As if anything you say matters now?" I took a step toward him. "As if we're friends?" I snarled.

Seeing him retreat at my advance was gratifying. "Yes, maybe, and no," he said, ticking the answers off on his fingers. "Do you want to hear what I have to say or not?"

I had the feeling that no matter what I said, he'd tell me anyway. "Fine." I plunged my hands into my pockets, curling my fingers into fists.

Asakku stayed silent for a moment, looking at the courtyard around us. "Aren't you cold?"

I glared at him, noticing that the snow was evaporating into steam as it hit his perfectly pressed suit coat. "Get to the point."

He sighed. "I didn't take the nail from you to give it to the one who was looking for it. I took it to hide it. You have no such capacity. Anywhere you put it would be at risk. I didn't know about the gar. If he can find an adequate place where it will be protected, I will gladly return it. It's what they're *for*, anyway."

A bitter, sharp laugh that tasted like broken promises left me. "What makes me think you're telling the truth?"

"I haven't lied to you once since we met. Everything I've said has been true—even if it's occasionally been… less than forthright." Asakku wasn't meeting my eyes. His posture looked tense. Drawn into himself. Now that I was studying him, I could tell he was hurt. He was favoring his left leg a little, and his back was stiff and straight as though trying to prevent the suit coat from lying against it.

An unexpected pang of sympathy sliced through me. I actually felt bad that he was hurt, no matter how angry I was at him. No matter how much I wanted to grab him and shake him. Or set him on fire. "You're injured."

Asakku laughed. "And?"

"Why?"

"That's not relevant."

I squinted at him.

"You're blue."

The statement took me off guard, and I frowned. "What?"

"Blue. Your lips. Your skin is paler than usual. You're cold."

Mirroring his response, I raised a brow. "And?"

"Will you smite me if I touch you?"

"I might."

"Fair enough." He closed the distance between us in a few steps and reached out. His hand rested on my shoulder, and heat poured through me from the contact. I hadn't realized how cold I was until that moment.

When I didn't attack him, he moved his hand to the center-left of my chest, over my heart and left it there, allowing the innate heat of him to pool into me. The warmth heated my heart, and the blood in it, which in turn warmed the rest of me.

Damn him for being right.

# CHAPTER 30

We stood there in silence for what felt like an eternity, me wrestling with the instinct to smite him and him warming me from the inside out. He didn't say anything, didn't move much, and seemed ready to jump away from me if I twitched. The feeling was mutual. It was, at best, an uneasy truce.

"Deceiving you brought me no pleasure," he said, echoing what he'd told me at the church. "But you would not have done what I needed you to do had I been honest. And I couldn't risk that. This was too important to be so cavalier."

I glared at him. He wasn't wrong, of course, but that didn't make him more trustworthy or this situation easier to accept. "So why tell me now?"

"Because I don't relish the idea of having you hunt me down. Or of fighting you. And if the junkyard dog you've been working with can find a safe place for the nail, that would be an improvement over my current options. Also, my intent was always to return it to you, but you were being hunted after the events at Old North Church. And you still are, which means it would be at risk if something happens to you."

"Why do you keep calling him that?"

"Hm?"

"Mister Graves."

"Well, the primary use of a gar is to protect a place, is it not? All snarling and slavering and ready to tear anyone not supposed to be there to shreds." Asakku waved a hand. "Feed it occasionally, and it will stay loyal forever."

His dismissal of Axton annoyed me, but then, everything about him did. "And I'm supposed to believe any of this?" I asked, still not sure if I wanted to throw a punch in his direction. I didn't trust his words, but at the same time, I didn't think he was lying. At least not about this.

When he judged me warm enough, Asakku lowered his hand and moved back and away from me again before I could settle on whether or not to hit him. "I will prove it in time. Besides, we both know a fight between us would be... unwise."

"You're already injured. I have the advantage," I pointed out.

"Perhaps, but it would be a Pyrrhic victory at best."

"A what?"

He sighed. "Uncultured. It means that whoever wins would be damaged badly enough—and maybe even dead—that it might not be worth it. Pyrrhus was a general a very, very long time ago. He won a war, but his entire army died. He might have, too, come to think of it." He tapped his lips with a manicured finger. "Either way, it means a fight that nobody will really win. Even the winner will lose."

I grunted. "Be that as it may, it may be worth it." My mind went back to the demon I'd fought in the drug lab the year before. Pyrrhic victory indeed.

"Perhaps, but is it worth it right this minute? If you and I kill each other, the nail will still be out of reach. And you will be unable to do further work, dear angel. As odious as I may be," his mouth twisted in a sardonic manner, "waiting until the hunt for you and your hound cools down benefits your goals just as it does mine."

Taking a long, deep breath, I ground my teeth in frustration. The worst part about this was he was right. Of course, they always were, weren't they. Back you into a corner, tie you in knots, then show you that it had been your own doing all along. The devil truly is in the details. "Fine."

Asakku smiled, his ember-colored eyes finally meeting mine. "You're smarter than you give yourself credit for. Truth be told, I wasn't sure how this was going to go. I'm pleased you saw reason. I'll be in touch." He vanished, leaving me alone again in the courtyard.

I could still feel the phantom warmth of his hand on my chest, and I reached to touch it. Still more waiting. Though his point about Axton and I being hunted was a good one. I pulled out my phone and flipped it open, fingers hovering over the keys as I considered whether or not to update Axton.

On the one hand, he should know about the development. Insomuch as there was one. Had Asakku really told me much other than that he was going to make contact again soon? I fought with myself over it, trying to decide what in the world to do with myself and with the situation.

No closer to an answer, I closed the phone with a click and put it back in my pocket and headed into shelter's back entrance, letting myself into the kitchen with my key. The space was dark and quiet. Dust must have left with Eirlas after bringing me the cocoa. I didn't see Jim anywhere, either. Or Axton.

I wandered through the kitchen and out into the dining area, sitting down at one of the tables. It was close to the time when T would be getting out of work. Part of me felt guilty for not having gone in today, but there was no way I could have with the church meeting happening that morning. It felt so much longer than a few hours ago, but a great deal had happened in a short span of time.

Axton was probably still angry with me about my outburst at the priest, too. But… I pulled my phone back out and opened it, calling his number before I could give myself too much time to think about it.

"Graves," he said after several rings.

"It's Cassiel."

He grunted. "Yeah?"

"The demon showed up again."

"You kill 'im?"

"No. He said he'd return the nail to us when things quiet down and we aren't being hunted. I'm not sure I believe that, but it's what he claimed."

Axton snorted. "Yeah, okay. And I've got a bridge to sell you."

"You own a bridge? I don't have much money."

There was a very long silence. "Thank you for making my point for me." Axton sighed over the line. "The point is you're an idiot if you believe him."

"What does that have to do with a bridge?"

Another long silence. Another sigh. He then hung up.

I returned home and arrived at the same time as T, who filled the silence by talking to me about some of the work he had that day and a phone call with his daughter. His grandkids were apparently enjoying their Christmas gifts that he'd bought them. I let him chatter on and interjected with appropriate responses now and then.

He cooked dinner but had me do some of the work of cutting vegetables or stirring things on the stove. It was nothing I hadn't done with Dust in the kitchen at the church. I wasn't much of a cook, though, and while I could do individual things, putting them all together was beyond me. I could follow a very detailed recipe step by step, but that was about the extent of it. By the end of it, we had made spaghetti and meat sauce.

We ate at the table, and eventually, T sat back in his seat, watching me with interest. "So, how did everything go with your work today?"

I had dreaded the question since he'd come home. "Disaster."

His expression became concerned, his heavy brows furrowing a little. "That bad, huh?"

"Nobody died that I know of, but we failed entirely."

"Hey, if nobody died, and you're all here to fight another day, that counts." T patted my arm, his hand broad and warm. "Sometimes, not dying is enough of a win." His tone was soft when he said that, and his eyes were a little distant.

"Maybe. Also, Dust and Eirlas are having issues with the priest at the church. I confronted him, but I am worried I only made things worse."

He asked about them, and I laid the situation out. A growling noise left him, and he shook his head. "That's bullshit."

"Yes. Bullshit," I repeated. I knew what it meant; I'd heard the word many times at the shelter. Eirlas had explained those words and their meanings and usages early on, though he'd cautioned me against using them.

T stared at me for a second, then laughed. "Now there's a thing to hear."

"I have heard some people think it is uncouth. Or sinful. It isn't sinful, of course, but neither are half the things people say are."

"Well, it's impolite anyway. Not sure it's a sin. Sorry. I try not to swear much in polite company."

"I am polite company?" That was the first time I'd ever been accused of such a thing, and I couldn't tell how I felt about it.

T scratched the back of his head, looking uncertain. "Well, I guess so. You're an angel. Probably the politest company I'll ever have."

"That is also bullshit."

T burst out laughing, and for a moment, I felt a little better.

# CHAPTER 31

It was several days before I heard from Asakku. I spent the time working at the shop and sending the occasional text to Axton and Jim to keep them up to date that there was nothing to keep up to date. T started teaching me more about fixing cars, and I soaked up the data like a sponge. I had never been one of the smarter angels, but working with my hands made sense to me. T was patient with my mistakes and only ever told me to do something again. The only time I saw him even remotely frustrated was when I broke something he then had to replace. Or didn't put his tools back where they belonged. Honestly, that annoyed him more than anything else.

Axton told me he'd gone to see Ruth, and she'd made some calls up the chain to people higher up in the church about Father Demoyne and had started the gears turning to have him reassigned. I didn't think reassignment was sufficient for the way he had behaved, myself. But I had no say in any of it, and Axton said the bureaucracy of the church was often slower to act than one might hope. Particularly since Father Demoyne hadn't broken any laws. Being an ass was, unfortunately, not cause for defrocking.

I didn't sleep well those few nights, and on the third day, I decided to take a walk after waking up from a nightmare that featured Father John's death and a loop of the fight with the demon who had killed him. Except this time, instead of shock numbing the pain I'd endured, I felt everything. The burns from the hellfire, the pain of his claws tearing me apart, the sound of his laughter. I lost the fight over and over again in my head.

The icy winter air cleared my mind a little when I stepped outside. A soft whisper of Grace told me I wasn't alone, and I looked around. Seeing nothing, I started my walk, and a moment later, Codiel appeared beside me, making me jump.

"I did not mean to startle you, sister," he said by way of apology.

I tried to will the knot of stress the startlement had caused away. Of all the people I had ever met, Codiel was, without a doubt, the least threatening. "I wouldn't have thought you did. Though I'm surprised to see you."

"I am always with you. But... you seemed troubled and in need of companionship."

A heavy sigh left me, steam curling out before us and then fading as I walked through it. "Maybe. I fear I made a mistake letting Asakku go. We both know demons cannot be trusted."

Codiel shook his head, his golden hair swaying a little as he padded along beside me in his bare feet, unbothered by the snow and cold. He still wore perfectly white robes, tied at the waist with a golden length of rope. I remembered wearing such things, but at this point, it was a faded thought after two years on Earth. "No, they cannot." His words pulled me out of my thoughts. "I do not have any wisdom to share about his motives. I wish I could, but... I am assigned to watch over *you*, not him."

"I know." The snow crunched under my sneakers. "I'm an idiot for giving him a chance, aren't I?"

His brows drew together, expression pensive. "It is not my place to judge, only to watch. But if it helps, I do not think you an idiot. It is not foolish to desire to see the best in others." Codiel looked at me. "It may not be the decision I think best in the case of a demon, but what I think does not matter much. This is your life, Cassiel. You must live it as you believe is best."

That didn't make me feel better, but I nodded anyway. I knew he couldn't really pass judgment on me either way. Watchers are, by nature, impartial. They don't have the luxury of opinions. Hell, it was unusual he interacted with me at all. I guessed the change was because I was both a fallen and because there was that purpose laid out for me. "Do you know what they wanted that nail for?"

"If I did, I am not sure I could tell you. But I do not." I knew Codiel couldn't lie, and he wouldn't know how to bend the truth, either. If he claimed not to know, that was the entire truth. In some ways, it was a relief to interact with another angel since, while I trusted my friends, sometimes I had learned that what they said and how they felt were not always the same. Creatures of the earth were squirrely like that. Even the good ones.

This time of night, the city was quieter than usual, and the constant hum of traffic had fallen to a low murmur. With the recent snowfall, it all seemed muffled somehow. Like even Boston was holding its breath. I crossed the main thoroughfare, waiting for the traffic signals to give me leave to go, and then continued onward. Codiel kept pace with me, not speaking but just "holding space," as Jim would have called it.

After several blocks of aimless wandering, Codiel touched my shoulder, giving me pause. "Take a left here," he indicated, pointing down another road. "There is an angry, drunken man on a bicycle ahead who will attempt to fight you if he sees you."

I followed his advice. "Thank you."

"Of course, sister." He smiled at me, and it was like the sun radiating warmth from the heavens. "Just because I cannot help you in all things does not mean I cannot help you in some."

I returned the smile. I couldn't not. It was like when Tiny jumped up to lick my face — I had no say in the matter. "I appreciate it."

We continued on in silence until I realized I had no idea where I was. I stopped to look around and noticed a bus stop and decided to take advantage of the flight platform to get airborne. While I can take off from the ground, it's always easier to have a start, and city planners know it. Many winged creatures cannot get airborne without one, in fact. So — in Boston, at least — they built platforms onto the overhang of bus stops. They are nothing but a set of stairs leading up to a dais about fifteen feet off the ground, but it helps.

I climbed the stairs, mindful of ice and fussed with my clothes, opening the closures in them to let my wings out, grateful for the clothing T had helped me purchase that accounted for exactly that. Even a mere fifteen feet above the street, the air was colder and felt like it moved faster, though perhaps that was my imagination. I called my wings out and splayed them, feeling the currents through my feathers. Codiel stood beside me, patient and watchful, and for some reason, I felt a need to explain. "I got turned around."

He shrugged. "You are not far from home. If you need, I can show you the way."

"I should be all right."

"You are certain?" he asked, tilting his head.

"Yeah." I can be a stubborn ass at times, and dealing with problems myself and eschewing assistance is one of my less appealing traits. I have never been good at accepting help from anyone. Maybe it's because I spent so long alone. Maybe it's trust issues. Maybe it's Maybelline. We'll never know.

"All right, sister. I will leave you to it. Remember, I am never far." He smiled and bowed his head, stepping aside to give me room to take off.

I leapt off the platform and caught the air, churning it with my wings as I gained altitude easily with the ocean wind blowing through the streets. As I flew higher, the city lay out before me and, to the east, the ocean. North was the huddle of skyscrapers that marked the center of Boston. I recognized their shape but had yet to learn the purpose of any of them.

With the snow, the painted names of the streets on the pavement below was hidden, making it harder to get my bearings, but I was in no real hurry. At the height I was, I let the wind hold me aloft and glided, making small corrections to stay up. The city felt very small from up there, and I was reminded that, for all its activity, the sheer number of people in it, and size, Boston was only one city in the scope of things.

Jim had shown it to me on a map on his phone once. He had started zoomed in to where we were at the time and then pulled out until I saw all of Boston. Then all of Massachusetts. Then all of New England. Then the United States, and on until we were looking at a satellite view of the entire planet. I had been floored. While from my vantage at the gates of Heaven I had known there was, of course, more than a mere single city down here, the scale felt very different when I was up close with it.

Whether it was the act of flight, which had always cleared my head, or the cold air or the perspective or my brother's company, I felt more settled than I had. Which brought with it fatigue and the need to sleep. I circled, looking down at the streets below as I tried to pick out landmarks I recognized until I found our building and descended toward it.

When I landed on the sidewalk, I felt the same sort of demonic taint I had every time Asakku was near. I had come to recognize it and wondered if it was, perhaps, him identifying himself. Telling me he was close without revealing his exact location. What his purpose for that could be, I didn't know, but I accepted it as one of his many eccentricities.

I looked around but saw nothing, though I still felt his presence close by me. After a good couple minutes, I quietly called his name, mindful not to disturb anybody in the surrounding buildings. It was, after all, very late.

A soft noise answered me. From what I could tell, it came from between my building and the one beside it, so I headed in that direction, my senses on high alert for danger. This could well be some sort of trap, but I, the fool, couldn't just ignore it.

I've never been the sharpest fish in the tree.

# CHAPTER 32

Asakku, in one of his tailored suits, sat on the ground against a dumpster, the slush around him crimson. He was breathing hard, his head lulled forward and steam billowing from his lips as he panted. Some part of me still wanted to smite him, but I ignored the impulse.

Caution faded, and I approached him, dropping down to a knee in the cold and wet. "Asakku," I said quietly touching his shoulder to try and rouse him.

He jumped, lifting his head, his hand snapping up and clawed fingers digging into my wrist. A snarl covered his features, but as recognition set in, the grip loosened, and his hand slid away. "Angel," he said wearily. "Forgive me."

"It's all right. What happened?" This whole situation felt too similar to my fall. Arazael coming to me wounded, saying he was being chased. My stomach churned, acid rising in my throat. This wasn't Arazael. I wasn't letting him into Heaven. This was Earth, and I still needed him, more or less, until he returned the nail to me.

Asakku clumsily fished a hand into his jacket and pulled out a bundle wrapped in a square of red silk, pressing it into my hand. I could feel the nail's Grace humming in resonance with mine the moment I laid a hand on it. "Keep it safe."

"Let me help you," I said without thinking, shoving the nail into my pocket. "You're hurt."

A bitter, tired chuckle escaped him. "We are meant to be enemies, Cassiel. You cannot heal me." He made no effort to move, however. As if he was just too tired to get up. "I'll be all right."

"You don't look all right." I looked around, realizing he couldn't have gone too far in this state. It was very possible that whatever had hurt him like this was in pursuit.

"I've survived worse," Asakku growled, shifting his weight and trying to stand. His Italian leather shoes weren't made for this kind of environment, and he struggled to gain purchase on the ground.

I put an arm under his and lifted him to his feet with very little effort. He didn't weigh much despite the fact that I could feel he was built quite solidly under the suit. Most angels are muscular and more or less perfect specimens of our species, and as an archdemon, Asakku still carried that. Or at least this form did. He could be a hideous beast masquerading as a mortal for all I knew. In fact, he likely was—Blight taints, violates, and twists all things, including one's appearance. Most demons' true forms are horrifying to behold. And I say that as someone who has siblings with nothing but eyes and wings.

He made a pained, annoyed sound when I lifted him, and I realized the back of his suit coat was shredded. My arm came away wet and red. As soon as he was upright, he put a hand on the dumpster and straightened with a grunt. "Be careful, angel. There are those who would take advantage of your giving nature."

While I knew he wasn't wrong, I couldn't ignore someone in pain like that any more than I could stop breathing. Even if he was a demon. Even if I did want to smite him to ashes. "Maybe," I said. "You should still seek medical attention."

"From whom?" he asked, his tone dripping with biting acrimony. "Just walk into a hospital and demand they see to me? Or perhaps your wounded Marine friend would stitch me up like he does you? I think not." Asakku lifted his burning, ember-colored gaze to mine. "I am not afforded such luxury. I will heal. Worry about yourself, angel. Having that thing puts you in the crosshairs, and there is only so much I can do to protect you. To that end, I've left you something upstairs under your bed. Show it to your dog; he can explain it. It will keep the nail safe."

The notion of Asakku, a demon, protecting *me* threw me off a little. I ignored his bad attitude and studied his tired, blood-flecked face, watching his eyes for a moment. He was tired. Hurting. Worried. It looked honest for all I could tell, as much as I didn't trust it. "I will see to it that this is safe. You have my word."

He nodded, closing his eyes as though in relief. "Good. I will see you around, Cassiel." Then he vanished as though he'd never been there but for a red stain on the ground and on my coat sleeve.

I took a moment to try and put the pieces together, but it felt like something was missing every time. First, he'd kept his word that he'd bring me the nail. For whatever that was worth—he could be playing a long game for all I knew. But an artifact like this didn't seem like it warranted a long game. He could have kept it and been probably better off for it.

Second, he'd apparently acted against his own self-interest in protecting the nail and, he claimed, me. Obviously, there were other demons looking for this artifact. That horde of them hadn't been under his control that I could tell. He struck me as the solitary sort, not a commander. Much as some angels were created for various jobs, as an archdemon, he would still be acting more or less in the purview he had. Just twisted. Broken.

Third, he'd been the one to bring this to my attention to begin with. If not for my involvement, that angry mob of people outside the Old North Church would have burned it to ashes, most likely, and could have made way for an incursion into the vault by a mortal convinced to do the demons' will. While only an archdemon can cross into sanctified space, mortals are easily bought and sold with money and have no such restrictions.

So what was the game? To make me trust him and then turn on me as some part of a bigger ploy? That could be the case, but for now, I didn't have enough information to make that leap. Suspicion or otherwise.

I pulled my phone out of my pocket and called Axton. He needed to know about the development, and Asakku was right—of everyone I knew, he was likely the only one who would be able to help me hide this effectively.

It took two calls and letting it ring for Axton to answer. "'Lo?" he growled into the phone, his voice rough with sleep.

"Axton, it's Cassiel."

"Th' fuck? It's," there was a rustle, "after two in the morning. This'd better be good."

"I have the nail."

There was a long pause and the sound of movement on his end. "Oh. Okay, this is good." He sounded more awake. "Where are you?"

"Home. I'm going to head to St. Mary's cemetery and meet you there. Sanctified ground. I don't know if anyone is hot on the trail here, but if they are, I shouldn't be too close to T's."

"Good call. I'll be there as quick as I can."

"All right. I'll see you shortly."

I left the alleyway at a jog, made my way to the roof, and took back to the air for the second time that night. The temperature had dropped, and the higher I got, the colder it became. A sharp, harsh wind was blowing from the north, and the clouds had thickened.

Right. The nor'easter. Father John had explained them to me when I had stayed with him during that first year. Massive storms that blow down the coast from the northeast. While they are most common in winter, they sometimes come during the summer and dump buckets of rain and spit lightning all the way from Maine to Virginia. Unique to the East Coast, they are vicious beasts of high winds and heavy precipitation.

Those same winds made it very difficult as I made for St. Mary's. It was normally less than ten minutes by air, but I kept getting blown off course and having to fight my way back. Worse, snow began to fall, obscuring my vision and turning the city into a haze of streets I had no names for. The cold cut through my coat and made my breathing come rougher. I had to pause a moment to try and get my bearings.

"Quickly, sister. You are in danger." Codiel's voice came from beside me, and I twisted that direction, squinting through the snowfall. "Follow," he commanded, a soft golden glow surrounding him as he took off in the opposite direction to where I'd been going.

Unlike my brother, for whom the wind and snow meant nothing, I struggled after him, my feathers beginning to ice over as snow landed on them and melted. I wasn't in danger of falling out of the sky, but it was far from easy. Having a guiding light to follow, however, made it possible to navigate.

I had neither time nor breath to ask him what I was in danger from, but I trusted his word implicitly. Codiel, unlike Asakku, couldn't lie. There were things he couldn't tell me and limits he had to adhere to, but his intentions were never in question: he followed the mandate of Heaven. Of the Father.

I recognized the pattern of the street lights as we approached the cemetery and began my descent, gliding in slowly decreasing circles. I couldn't go straight in with the wind or I risked being blown into one of the trees or monuments.

"Watch out!" Codiel's voice distracted me, and I looked around for the threat just in time for a weight to land on my back, driving me toward the ground.

# CHAPTER 33

I flailed, trying to control my descent as the weight on my back drove me downward. I was about fifty feet above the ground at that point and could barely make out the snow-covered graves rushing up to meet me.

Tucking my wings in close, I rolled to the side sharply and threw them open again, dislodging my unwelcome guest. A dark shadow harried me. I couldn't make it out against the black sky, but the movement caught my attention as it circled. My opponent was faster than I, but that didn't surprise me. I am a shield, not an arrow.

Another blow came, this time on my left wing as the figure tried to destabilize me a second time. I folded my wings and rolled again, giving up on any attempt at a slow descent. Instead, I dropped like a rock toward the ground until the very last moment I could. I then snapped my wings open, cupping them and straining to slow to a reasonable speed so I wouldn't splatter against the ground. Or, worse, a gravestone. I had done that once already last year when Jim, Eirlas, and I had taken shelter in the vault there after demons had attacked St. Mary's and had no desire for a repeat performance.

It seemed to be a recurring theme. Demons attacking churches; me hiding in cemeteries. I wasn't in the mind to consider what that meant at the moment, however.

I landed hard, narrowly avoiding hitting a stone cross, and jogged several steps, my shoes sliding in the gathering snow but not badly enough to knock me over. At least this time, I hadn't broken anything in my mad dash for the shelter of sanctified ground.

Undeterred, the figure dove on me from above, striking me in the back and knocking me forward. Claws raked my shoulders through my coat, and I yelled in protest, reaching back and finding shredded, damp fabric. I leaned forward, rolling my shoulders and yanking, flipping my assailant over me and onto the ground at my feet.

Asakku snarled, his eyes wild with feral outrage. I hadn't recognized him before, and now that I saw him, something in the pit of my stomach tightened. Of course it was him. His wings were splayed out to either side, sickly looking black things missing far too many feathers. He shouldn't have been able to fly like that.

He stood so quickly, I couldn't register the movement and lunged, his claws outstretched toward me. It was a clumsy motion that didn't fit with the polished, focused man I'd come to recognize. I sidestepped the attack, grabbing his arm and throwing him past me using his own momentum. For an archdemon, he fought like a feral beast with no tactical awareness or forethought.

He fell over a gravestone, slipping and colliding with it hard enough that I grimaced in instinctual sympathy as he bent over the thing and slid to the side. Asakku taking a moment to recover gave me time to realize what was missing. He wasn't using hellfire. He wasn't even using his mind, so far as I could tell. Asakku had always had several irons in the fire and had been several steps ahead of me since we'd met. Everything was a chess game for him. Everything.

So what had changed?

Asakku grabbed his head as though he'd struck it, though he'd hit the headstone at waist height. His back was still bleeding, coloring the snow he'd landed in. "Stop it!" he snarled. "Stop it, damn you!"

I moved toward him, taking the opening and grabbing his wrists, dragging him with me and pinning him against one of the stone monuments that towered above the others. Somebody or other important had been buried there and needed to tell the world how important they'd been.

His cry of pain made something in my chest ache. "What is going on here, Asakku?" I demanded, using his own fatigue and weakness against him as I held him in place. Normally, I wasn't certain I could have done such a thing without breaking parts of him, but he'd lost enough blood that his struggles were feeble. His wings flailed some as he squirmed.

"Let me go!" He bared his teeth at me like a wild animal. His gaze looked feverish, his eyes glassy as though he were high or ill. "I will tear you limb from limb."

His Blight felt different somehow as he railed against me. I could feel it clashing with my Grace, our power almost striking sparks against one another. It wasn't the same. Something was overshadowing him, making him dance like a marionette to a tune he didn't want to hear. I could feel the two energies roiling over one another like two cats in a fight, tumbling and clawing and shredding one another so quickly and so hard that it was almost impossible to tell where one began and the other ended.

I didn't recognize the other presence, but the scope of it terrified me. I had no idea what or who was pulling his strings, but it was on a scale I had never experienced.

With this new realization, I shifted from trying to fight him to simply trying to hold him still. I released his wrists and wrapped my arms around his torso, my wings pressing up against his as I held him close and tight. "Come on, Asakku. Fight it. Fight him."

Asakku's claws went straight through my coat and into my back, driving hard into my skin, but he didn't shred me this time. Instead, it felt like he was holding on. His head turned, and he sunk fanged teeth into my neck, making me groan as blood rushed over my skin. Unlike vampires, he didn't feed on blood or any such thing, so his bite lacked any of the analgesic qualities of vampire saliva. It just hurt.

"I have you," I said, my voice rough with pain. "I have you."

His chest heaved with snarling breaths as he waged an internal war against the invading force, clinging to me with everything he had. Like I was salvation somehow.

I had no idea how long we stood there with the snow gathering on me and melting off him. Holding him like that was like embracing a furnace. He was so hot, it almost burned. At least I wouldn't end up hypothermic, I thought. Small mercies. My knees trembled, and we slid down the monument together, me not willing to risk letting him go as he fought whatever was happening inside him.

As we knelt together, entangled, I prayed for mercy, for peace. Whatever grace could be afforded him, I pled for. Demon or not, I took no pleasure in his pain and torment.

Using my Grace would burn him, and I wasn't sure if I could risk trying to pick at the snarl of Blight that had him caged without killing him. Unsure what else to do, I begged the Father for help or intercession. Something.

Anything. Tears of frustration, fatigue, and physical pain rolled down my cheeks since Asakku's claws had plunged deep into the muscles in my back, his Blighted presence burning down into them.

It felt like an eternity before Codiel appeared near me, moving with purpose and focus. He knelt at my side in the snow, putting a hand to the top of my head. *"Free him,"* he whispered in Enochian. Not knowing if I could or how I would even go about that, I hesitantly called on my Grace before reaching into Asakku and trying to catch the threads of control that had been coiled so tightly around his spirit.

A pale blue glow cast eerie shadows on the headstones around us as I worked, the light tinged with Codiel's warm, golden energy. I could feel him pouring power into me as I worked, him acting as a conduit for something so much bigger than either of us directly.

When I found what I sought, I gripped the tether in hand and used the well of combined Grace to try and sever the thread. As if it were a conscious, living thing, the power recoiled from me, releasing Asakku and whipping back away into inky darkness not even my power could dispel alone. Grace may be more powerful than Blight innately, but there's still something to be said for sheer volume.

Asakku screamed through his grip on my neck, his muscles coiling tighter as if to instinctively fight the power I used while simultaneously having the effect of drawing him closer. Like a moth to flame. The pain was distant by then. Present, but not in the forefront of my mind as I focused on the surgical precision I needed to avoid killing him outright while I used my Grace to unsnarl his soul from the grip of… whoever that had been. Asakku himself was straining against the compulsion like an animal caught in a trap, ready to gnaw off its own limbs to escape. Feeling his will's frantic struggle only bolstered my belief that I was making the right decision.

When the last tendril fled from me, and I surfaced from the intense focus I had been using, I realized the snow around us had melted, and Asakku was steaming. He sagged in my arms, claws sliding free of my skin, jaw unclenching. I worried I'd gone too far and done too much, but just as I was ready to lay his limp body down, he roused himself to speak.

"You should ha-have smote me," he murmured in a broken voice, resting his head on my shoulder as he gathered his faculties. "Why didn't you?"

"You weren't really fighting me. Not for real." I grimaced as my body registered the punctures of his teeth and claws, and the blood on the side of my neck started to freeze against my skin in the icy air. "It wasn't you."

"Are you so sure?" he said, his tone a weakly cocky mimicry of his usual manner. "I've wanted to sink my teeth into you for a while now, just... not quite like that."

"Yes." I didn't rise to the baiting comment.

He grunted. "I... suppose I should thank you."

I managed a smile. "I'm told that's polite."

A wheezing chuckle escaped his lips as he pulled back from me. "Thank you, angel. I should go before your junkyard dog arrives. I doubt he would be so, mn, merciful."

"Who was it?"

His tired, pained gaze met mine. "I cannot say." The words had the ring of truth about them. No dancing around it. No deception. No flowery words.

I nodded. "Maybe someday, you will." And by "maybe" and "someday," I meant he would and soon.

"Maybe." Asakku groaned as he stood, plunging his hands into his pockets. In the shadows of the graveyard, he looked more like a shade than a person except for the burning glow of his eyes. "I'll see you around, angel." He then staggered off among the stones, perhaps too tired to pull his vanishing act.

I watched him go, staring in that direction until I heard footsteps at a run off to my left. I tensed, peering in that direction, and splaying my wings as I forced myself to my feet.

Axton came up beside me, a gun clutched in his hand, his expression hard and cold as he surveyed the churned up and bloody snow. His eyes raked over me and then back out at the rest of the graveyard. "You're bleeding."

"Yep."

"Wanna fill me in on that, or...?"

"Nope."

"Damn it, Cass," he growled, glaring at me. "What the hell is going on?"

I pulled the nail—still in the Royal Crown bag—out of my pocket and unwrapped it from the silk pocket square. "Here."

He grimaced when I offered it to him, his eyes screwing up and mouth tightening as though it were too bright and perhaps stunk. Axton took it and shoved it in his pocket. "Great, but what aren't you telling me, huh? I don't want anything to do with this shit as it is, and now you're keeping secrets."

I sighed, holding the scrap of silk to the side of my neck where I was still bleeding. "I got attacked on my way here. We knew there were demons after this thing." I didn't know why I was loathe to tell him about my brawl with Asakku. Or why I felt like I needed to defend him.

"On holy ground?" he asked.

I pointed up. "It landed on me up there, and we went down together." That was mostly true. "I'm not sure if it knew this was sanctified ground or not or if it was just suicidal."

"How couldn't it know?"

I shrugged some, feeling the claw marks to my back and shoulders pull. "Nobody said they were smart."

That seemed to mollify Axton for now, but I could feel him staring. "Uh-huh." His tone was noncommittal enough to be polite, but I knew better. "You going to be okay?" he asked, gaze flicking to the bite mark on my neck.

"Yeah. I think I just need a shower and some sleep," I replied, rubbing my bloody hands over my face and leaving streaks. "Maybe two showers."

Axton made a sound that could have been a laugh. "You want a ride home? We can talk on the way."

I looked up at the clouds and shivered a little, not relishing the idea of trying to make it in the air. "Yeah."

He jerked his chin toward the front of the cemetery, and we walked together in silence, our shoes crunching the snow underfoot.

# CHAPTER 34

I shivered as I flopped into the passenger seat and closed the door. Axton joined me and started the car, turning on the heat. He hadn't left it off long, so the engine was still warm. "I'd hoped to have this talk on sanctified ground," he said, pulling away from the curb. "But something tells me that sanctified ground is of limited help at this point."

My head leaned back into the seat, and I closed my eyes. "The one after it is definitely powerful enough that it is of no consequence to him," I said, thinking of the vast, boiling well of power that had been controlling Asakku. A tremble that had nothing to do with cold worked its way down my spine.

"You want to tell me about it, or should I just keep guessing?" Axton said, never once taking his eyes off the road as he crept down the street.

"I have no idea who it is," I said honestly. "I've never faced anything like it. It…" I sighed, searching for words and cussing my limited vocabulary.

I was silent for so long that Axton grunted. "I speak Enochian, you know."

I hadn't known. I switched languages. "It felt like a vast pool of Blight. The creature had control of a vessel and was using it to attack me indirectly. Such a being could only be an incredibly powerful archdemon. Perhaps another seraph. There is no way it could be anything lesser. It could even have been the Morning Star himself." The words came out in a rush. "It felt like a maelstrom of power all churning and boiling around a single point, reaching out to pull the vessel's strings." It felt odd to speak Enochian with someone who wasn't an angel, and I wasn't sure how I felt about it. That said, it did give me the ability to express everything more clearly.

Axton nodded slowly. "This vessel—it was a demon, I assume?" He spoke in English, but I could tell he understood what I'd said.

"Yes. An archdemon, though not a seraph. Perhaps a cherub once. I don't know for sure."

Another nod. "That's worrying, to say the least. And explains why it didn't just... combust when it hit the ground in the cemetery."

"To say the least," I echoed. "I am..." I took a breath, "afraid."

"You'd be an idiot not to be," Axton affirmed. "I'm not comfortable with the idea myself. That means this was part of something bigger. It's not just this one artifact. Something like that? It has its fingers in a lot of pies."

I frowned. "Why would having its fingers in a pie be helpful? How could it manage that? I'm not certain you could put that many close together, and—"

"It's a saying."

"Oh." My nemesis: *Vernacular*.

"What I'm saying here, Cass, is that it's doing a lot of different things at once to try and play the world's biggest game of chess."

That analogy, I understood. I had never played chess myself, but I understood a little of it. Eirlas and Jim liked to play together, and Jim had explained it to me as a game of strategy. A war analogue. "So why hasn't Heaven stepped in to stop it?" I asked, frowning as I tried to wrap my head around the idea.

Axton risked a glance at me. "Maybe it is."

Uncomfortable with the implication, I fell silent, and Axton didn't fill the space with talk. Instead, he turned on the radio and let it play while we crept through the city streets toward home.

When we arrived, I remembered the package Asakku had left for me. "Oh. I am to show you something."

Axton raised a brow at me.

"Asakku said you would understand."

He grunted and parked outside my building. "You want me to come up?"

"It may be best."

"I don't wanna wake your friend."

"He sleeps deeply."

Axton nodded once, and we disembarked, heading inside and up the stairs.

I opened the door to the apartment and crept in, pointing to the kitchen. It was the furthest from T's bedroom, and if we kept our voices down, it shouldn't wake him. Axton took my meaning and headed that way while I split off and headed into my room and removed my coat.

It hurt, and my shirt was stuck to my back with drying blood, though I could feel the punctures and tears had already begun to heal. While Asakku was a being of Blight, he hadn't been using it against me as a weapon, so the wounds weren't as desperate as the hellfire injuries I'd sustained in the warehouse.

I reached under the bed and pulled out the package Asakku told me he'd left me, half surprised it was actually there, and returned to the kitchen, where I flicked on the lights and handed it to Axton. "He said you would know how to use this and what it is."

"Great." Axton sat at the table and opened the package. It proved to be what looked like a very old wooden crucifix with the depiction of Christ crafted in gold. The whole piece was about the length of my arm—easily large enough to hide the nail. His brows rose, and Axton whistled low through his teeth. "I think I know what this is. But I very, *very* much want to know where your… 'friend'… got ahold of one of these."

He turned the crucifix over in his hands, pushing a small portion of the main body of the item down and away from him. It slid open, revealing a long, narrow space inside.

"Yep," he confirmed, nodding. "This is exactly what I thought it was."

I leaned over him and looked at the empty space within, recognizing Enochian sigils burned into the wood inside. They were wards for binding, obscuration, and dampening. I am no mage, and I know very little of magic in general, but even I recognized the purposes of the sigils. This item had been made to hide a powerful object.

Axton produced the nail from his pocket and opened the bag, pouring the iron nail into his palm. He rolled it between his fingers for a moment, staring at it with an expression I couldn't read. A moment later, he slid the nail into the hidden compartment. It fit like the crucifix had been made for it. He then closed the compartment, and the power of the nail winked out, vanishing from my perception. While the cross itself held some measure of Grace from the enchantment, it was infinitely more subtle than the nail itself had been.

He handed me the crucifix. "Take this and hide it somewhere only you will know about. The world doesn't need this kind of thing rattling around in it where just anybody can get their hands on it."

I frowned. The crucifix was as long as my arm, and the ornate golden figure on the front was instantly recognizable. Not to mention it was heavy. "I haven't the faintest idea where I could put this, Axton."

"Well, come up with something. And don't tell me, or anyone else, where you put it." He stood up. "I'm going back home to get some sleep. You should get cleaned up and do the same. You look like shit."

"Do I smell that foul?" I frowned and looked down at myself. I had showered the day before. Perhaps I had stepped or landed in something?

"Saying. But… yeah. You reek like demon blood." Axton pushed the chair he'd been sitting in back in to the table. "Call me when you have that thing hidden. And give me an update on the situation at the church, will you? I'm kind of invested."

I nodded. "I will. Thank you, Axton. For everything."

He looked at me and smiled a little. "It's my job. And Jim's a good guy." I noticed he didn't say anything about me. I didn't blame him; his dislike of anything related to the church wasn't unfounded. Axton made his way out, and I locked up after him before dragging myself into the shower to wash the blood off.

The hot water stung on the open wounds, as did the soap, but I'd endured far worse in my life, and being clean and warm was very worth it. My mind wandered to Ether and Maggie under the bridge as it often had on nights like this. Maybe I'd be able to do something to help them soon.

I leaned my head and arms onto the wall of the shower and stood in the steam, closing my eyes. At least it was over. The nail was more or less safe now, and whatever plan that other demon had for it was waylaid. I should have felt more at ease. Triumphant, even. Despite all, I had succeeded. So why did I feel so hollow?

One thing I did know, however, was someone was still listening to me. Father hadn't ignored my prayers or my plight. And if He hadn't ignored my request to help Asakku then… perhaps I was right. Perhaps he could be redeemed. Either that, or Asakku was part of some plan bigger than I could understand right now. I didn't know.

Whatever it was, this was just another sign on the road suggesting that, as bumbling as my progress was, it wasn't in the wrong direction. I hoped.

# CHAPTER 35

F ather Demoyne was transferred in under a week, and I took advantage of the change over to replace the crucifix that previously hung behind the altar in St. Mary's with the one that hid the nail. I could think of nowhere better to put it, and being inside the sanctuary of the church gave it an extra measure of protection beyond the dampening effect of the crucifix itself. The old crucifix I put in the priest's office, hanging it on the wall in an open spot. Nobody noticed in the shuffle.

The new priest, Father Carter, was a bright-eyed young human male who told everyone this was his first appointment. After a meeting with the heads of staff, he immediately reversed Father Demoyne's policies at the shelter and allowed Dust to reinstate his breakfast service for those staying there. He also went out of his way to tell Dust and Eirlas that he was proud to have such dedicated and obviously caring volunteers, and their relationship was their own business.

I liked him.

He was no Father John, but the youthful energy he brought to the ministry and to the church itself made all the difference. That, and he seemed to genuinely love the community. Apparently, he had grown up not far from there, so he knew the neighborhood and understood the importance of the programs Father John had pioneered, so Father Carter started drawing up more ideas for community outreach and expanding the budget for those things. Jim emerged from the meeting with a broad grin and told me about their plans.

I settled in with T and continued learning how to fix cars. It was a relief to work on problems that had concrete solutions, even if they weren't always easy. During that time, I began to understand the satisfaction that the Son found in carpentry. It was a different vocation, maybe, but working with my hands and making all the pieces fit felt good. I doubted I'd ever be a master mechanic like T was, but at the very least, I could make his work load lighter and pay him back for allowing me to stay with him.

That, and the money he paid me helped. I got the tattoo I wanted. Eirlas booked it for me with somebody he knew wouldn't ask too many questions or expect me to show ID. After a discussion about what I wanted and where, the artist did a few designs, and I soon had a replica of the cocktail umbrella Father John had given me on my left forearm near my elbow. The tattoo was even in color, though I was told the yellow ink might have trouble with fading over time. Apparently, it was a difficult color to apply.

The rest of the money I spent on purchasing things for the community under the bridge. I stopped by one evening, laden with gifts for the group. They welcomed me with surprise. Even Ether smiled.

"Well, look at you. I'd have figured you'd forget us," she said, accepting the package of wool socks I handed her.

"'What you do for the least of these, you do for Me,'" I answered.

"I have no idea what that's supposed to mean."

Maggie spoke up. "It's from the Bible, Ether. It means that taking care of people who don't have anything is important."

It was an imperfect explanation, but good enough that I didn't argue and continued passing out socks and sleeping bags with T's help. The people there had been uncertain of him at first, but his broad grin and the warmth and kindness that radiated out of him put everyone at ease.

"I ordered pizzas," T said as I walked past him. "We can't solve their problems, but everything's better with pizza."

I smiled at him. "You are a blessing," I said. And I meant it. While I hadn't known him long, his quiet, steady faith and genuine love were already a balm on my soul. As much as I loved Jim and the others, T had a way about him they didn't. Something I couldn't quite put my finger on.

T blushed and waved me off. "Bah, shaddup."

When the pizza arrived, we shared it with them, making merry of the dark Boston winter evening. It felt almost like a celebration, though of what, I couldn't say.

The following day when I went to the church, Dust stopped me at the door. "Hey, Cass, did you accidentally order something on the computer?"

I blinked a few times, taken aback. "I don't know how to use that foul thing."

"Okay, but I just received a shipment with your name on it."

My confusion deepened, and I shrugged. "I haven't ordered anything."

Dust wore a similarly perplexed expression and gestured for me to follow. He led me into the storage room, where a pallet of mustard jars sat. "I have no room for it, and this mustard is… easily a couple hundred bucks a jar. And there's no record anywhere of anyone at the church ordering it. The delivery guy said this was the address and verified that it was in your name, but…"

I stared at the mustard for a very long time and then smiled some. "Is it good mustard?"

"I mean, it's the most expensive mustard on the planet."

Laughter bubbled up in my throat and chest, and I covered my mouth. "Oh."

Dust looked at me askance, his expression suggesting he was worried I was losing my mind. Which only made me laugh harder. "It's a… a joke," I wheezed between giggles.

"That's an incredibly expensive joke."

His incredulity only made it funnier, and I staggered out of the room holding my sides. If nothing else, the demon had a sense of humor.

E. Prybylski has been in the publishing industry as an editor since 2009, starting at Divertir Publishing and eventually partnering with their close friend Richard Belanger to begin Insomnia Publishing.

Ever since childhood, E. has been an avid reader and writer of fantasy. The first chapter book they remember reading is The Hobbit, followed swiftly by most of Anne McCaffrey's Pern series. In high school, they perfected the skill of walking while reading without slamming into anyone. Mostly.

When they aren't reading or writing, E. is an active member of the Society for Creative Anachronism and has a B.A. in European history from SNHU. In addition to her many historical pursuits, E. is a musician of multiple instruments, a cat mom, and a loving wife to their husband, J. E. also speaks out for the disability and chronic illness communities being a sufferer of chronic migraines and Ehlers-Danlos Syndrome.

E's blog is located at ThirteenCentsShort.com